I0451750

ENGINES OF RUIN

by Lucas Magnum

The girl approached the church entrance. The door opened without her touching it. She drifted through and the door closed behind her. He broke into a run, almost face-planted in the gutter across from the church, righted himself and trotted up the salted church steps. The bells were drowned out by the sound of an organ, but the tune was unlike any church song he'd ever heard. The organist was leaning on a chord, sounding like he or she was grinding their fingers into the keys. It was minor. Diminished. Weird. His stomach sank. His mouth went dry.

He pushed open the door to the church. Reverend Gorman stood at the pulpit, petting the head of a lamb. Behind him was a mural depicting a nude woman levitating above a sea of roiling waves. The organist had stringy black hair that covered their face. Every few seconds their shoulders rolled forward as pressure was reapplied to the chord. The pews were full of the old and decrepit. Wrinkled eyes agog. Lizard lips hung open, leaking drool.

The girl was nowhere to be found. Harrison looked over his shoulder, thought about running outside, but the reverend's voice concussed the PA system and Harrison froze.

"Our Lady of the Sea," he said. "You've rained a generous bounty upon us in the time since the flood, in the years since we turned back to you in fear and love. Look upon us, your lonely congregation. Have pity and look with favor on our sacrifice."

Harrison turned back to the altar. He had to see for himself, even though he knew damn well blood would be spilled.

Gorman pulled a curved dagger from his vestments.

"Find favor with us, O Lady," he said.

He dragged the blade across the lamb's throat. Blood dyed the wool red. The lamb jerked its head side to side, gagging as it screamed. Gorman's eyes rolled back in ecstasy. He raised the blade. Looked to the heavens. The mural of waves began to move. The nude woman smiled.

Copyright © 2019 by Lucas Magnum
ISBN 978-1-949914-34-4
All rights reserved. No part of this book may be used or reproduced in any manner
whatsoever without written permission except in the case of brief
quotations   embodied in critical articles and reviews
For information address Crossroad Press at 141 Brayden Dr., Hertford, NC 27944
A Macabre Ink Production -Macabre Ink is an imprint of Crossroad Press.
www.crossroadpress.com

First Revised Edition

Preface to the New Edition

What you hold in your hand (or on your e-reader) is the culmination of nearly a decade's worth of work. I've wanted to be an author for most of my life, starting with the first time I saw a Stephen King movie on Halloween when I was six years old, but the truth is, I didn't really start trying until 2010 or so, after I met Jonathan Maberry. Something about his energy and work ethic made something in me click, and save for a serious six-month bout of depression earlier this year, I've been writing every day. I've never really looked back. This collection was an opportunity for me to do that.

A previous edition of this was published in October, 2017. I was desperate to get these stories out in the world as a collection, so I self-published it. While self-publishing doesn't bear quite the stigma it did in years past, I learned pretty quickly that it wasn't for me. I care far too much about the writing side to be filling my time (and spending money I didn't have) on designing covers, setting up ads, and hiring editors. It's just not in my personality. That's not to say I don't understand the business side of writing; it's just that my strengths (and passions) lie on the production end of things. I like putting words together to make sentences, and using those sentences to tell stories. And I think I'm good at it, but maybe I'm a little biased.

Last summer, Paul Goblirsch was kind enough to publish this collection as a limited edition hardcover. It sold out rather quickly (indeed, before I even knew it was available), and I wanted to get a paperback and e-book back on the market, but I didn't want to self-publish it again. Enter Brian Keene. At Killer Con in Austin, we chatted at the hotel bar, and when I brought up my collection, he suggested Crossroad Press. Though I was familiar with the publisher because they'd done reprints of many beloved horror titles of old, I hadn't considered them, because frankly I didn't think I was well-known enough.

I reached out to David Niall Wilson at Crossroad a few days after Killer Con, and was subsequently rewarded for my efforts. Sometimes you've just got to knock on the right doors. After some discussion, we decided the right thing to do, since the work was previously published, would be to add new content. There are five new stories. "Ghost Music," "Worm Magic," "Hayride," and "The Last Easy Rider" have never been published in any form. A very different version of "Offerings" was published in the anthology *crappy shorts: deuces wild*, but I think the version collected here is much better.

Revisiting this work has been fun and nostalgic, heartbreaking and rigorous. Most of all, it's reignited my love of the short story. I truly believe that not every idea is worth an eighty thousand-word manuscript. Sometimes, it only warrants eight thousand. Sometimes, it warrants even less than that.

I would like to think there's something for everyone here. That is, everyone who likes their fiction to be less about wish fulfillment and more about nightmares come true. There are horror stories. There are crime stories. There are stories that even I, the writer, have a hard time categorizing.

What I can say is that all of them were an absolute blast to write.

I hope they're just as much fun to read.

Lucas Mangum
Keeping it weird in Austin, TX

CONTENTS

Ghost Music

I get the call when I'm balls deep inside the third girl I've fucked that day. Of course, I ignore it. It can't be that important, at least not more important than getting off again. But then, whoever it is calls a second time, and a third, and by then I can't concentrate on fucking, so I pull out of the nameless girl and tell her to finish herself off if she needs to, otherwise she can just go.

She steps into her panties, pulls on a shirt and gathers her jeans. On the way to the door, she calls me an asshole, but I ignore her. She wouldn't be the first girl to call me that. Sure as shit won't be the last.

As the door slams behind her, I answer the phone, not bothering to get dressed (I rarely do these days). It's the first woman to call me an asshole, and the only woman I've ever really loved: the mother of my child who wasn't really a child anymore. Last I heard, my son was following in my footsteps, starting a band in that Godforsaken town I'd left behind one rainy night in a drunken stupor.

I half-expect her call is so she can taunt me about my highly publicized breakup with actress Shelby Andrews. It wouldn't be unlike her. She'd already had a grand old time teasing me over the ten-year age difference.

"Bernadette," I said. "To what do I owe the pleasure?"

"Please don't joke with me, Chase. It's not a good time."

Her voice held a familiar quality. She was trying very hard not to cry. I softened my tone and asked her if everything was okay, knowing damn well everything was not.

She then proceeded to tell me that our son had gone missing, just like so many of our friends had gone missing that summer my band recorded our debut EP in the Wheeler House. Bernadette had been pregnant then, and I was psychically torn between wanting to give it all up for the sake of fatherhood and making one last desperate attempt at rock stardom. In my seventeen-year-old mind, it was one or the other. I couldn't possibly do both.

"You've called the police?"

Now I was the one struggling to fight back a flood of emotion. I tried to tell myself that Hunter was probably okay. Probably ran off with a girl. Or maybe went off to play a show or record an album without telling his mother. But a niggling fear told me otherwise.

"How long has he been missing?"

"Three days."

"And you waited to tell me?"

"You have your own life now. I figured…"

"He's still my son."

"Chase. I'm scared."

"What can I do?"

"Don't make me say it."

"I'll come home."

"Thank you."

And then she did start to cry, right before she disconnected with me.

I arrived in Burgundy Woods the very next day. On the redeye from Los Angeles to Philadelphia, during a fitful, fragmented sleep, I dreamed of strange green lights in the windows of the old Wheeler place and a girl with black eyes, black because we burned them out with cigarettes.

You'd think running out on my family was the worst thing I've ever done. I wish that were true.

Her name was Madison Carli Byrd and she was a grade A cunt, a bad cliché, a musician's girlfriend who fucked all his friends and played them all against each other, but she didn't deserve to die. I didn't come to that realization with age and experience. I knew then that she didn't deserve what we did to her, but I went along with it. I share the guilt with all the founding members of my band, all of whom are dead now. Somehow I've managed to escape with my life, but that isn't to say I haven't suffered. I've paid dearly for my sins.

Of course, I have no way of knowing if I've paid in full. And that's what worries me most: that whoever's keeping the books has decided it's Hunter's turn to pay for my wrongdoing. I worry that she's still out there, seeking her revenge. Maybe Hunter's disappearance is her way of calling me back.

At Bernadette's doorstep, I drop my bags and pause a long while before knocking. When I finally do, she opens the door wearing a gray tank top, sweatpants, and no makeup. Her sandy hair is loosely tied and wisps of it hang free. Despite her uncared-for state, she still looks good to me and I feel a deep longing, one I knew I damn well couldn't avoid if I saw her again. On paper, I left her and Hunter to pursue my career, but the truth is I was hoping to protect them. I never stopped loving either of them, and deep down, I always imagined I would come home.

They say you can never go home again, meaning that places change in your absence; they cease to be your home during the time you are gone. But in Burgundy Woods, that's not exactly true, at least not for me. This place has been waiting for me. I see it in the small businesses that have survived the erection of a Walmart in the next town, the dusty sweet smell of the trees that still line most of the streets, and the way Bernadette pulls me into a shaky embrace and we make love like two mile-high club members trying to squeeze out one last desperate cramped bathroom quickie before the plane goes crashing into jagged, unforgiving mountains. Her cunt alone is like home, a cunt I've tried so fucking hard to forget, by drowning its memory in booze and snorting myself into dimensions where it doesn't exist and fucking as many other cunts as I can, hoping to find one just as warm and welcoming. But I never do, and I know without her telling me that she's never found a more perfectly fitting cock. That's not me making a boastful statement about my dick. I simply mean to say it's as if our genitals were crafted together, lock and key both parts of the same lot. We climax together and she tells me that she's made up the guestroom, but

I can stay with her.

"Do you want me to?"

"Don't make me say it."

I agree by saying nothing else and we fall asleep in each other's arms and I dream of a burning, empty stage, my distorted voice singing acapella over an invisible PA.

If I was to start somewhere, I figured it should be where it all came to an end. The Wheeler House. Everything began and ended there. With me. With Bernadette. With my band. With Madison and her vengeful spirit.

I don't remember the first time I learned of the house's existence, only that I first knew it as a source for many local legends, whispered about in the hallways of my school, referenced in cryptic sewer channel graffiti, and documented across digital forums dedicated to the paranormal. It was said that the house had been built over one of the seven gateways to Hell, that many grisly murders had taken place within its walls, though I only knew of one, and if it had occurred at a gateway to Hell, then that sure explained a lot of what followed. Maybe it had even been Hell that caused us to carry out that terrible deed.

I don't know for sure. All I know is if the spirit of Madison Carli Byrd has taken my son, then there is only one place he could be.

We took Madison to the Wheeler House under the pretense of letting her record backing vocals on one of our songs, a prospect she ate up just the way she ate up the fact that we were recording our EP in the haunted house to begin with.

There were seven of us that night: me and Bernadette, Madison of course, my guitarists Brian and Jade, Bob my bassist, and Gemma my drummer. The idea to sacrifice Madison was originally put forth by Jade as a joke, but then Brian started to really push for the idea. He said the devil would give us what we want if we made some sort of offering, and what was the harm in putting down a manipulative bitch like Madison anyway? He'd always had an interest in the occult, and he hated Madison much more than all of us did, though she had hurt all of us in equal. And while I have no evidence save for my own recollection of my thoughts at the time, I think we all were willing to give deals with the devil a try. We'd tired of playing lame top 40 covers in the dive bars peppered throughout our dead-end town like a plague of boils.

Now, unlike that fateful night, I enter the Wheeler House alone, but like that fateful night, I enter through the same half-boarded broken window on the north side of the property. I shimmy through, slowed by the excess flab I've accumulated over the last fifteen years. There isn't much of it thanks to poor nutrition and an excess of blow, but there's enough to make fitting through tight spaces more uncomfortable.

I tumble to the floor, raising a cloud of dust and rattling several shards of broken glass. I get up and look around, dusting myself off as I do so. The place hasn't changed very much. I'm in one of the bedrooms, the one that had supposedly belonged to little Peggy Wheeler, the final victim of her father, notorious serial killer Bradley Wheeler, who had strangled the life from somewhere between fifteen and thirty-five women when he was supposed to be out selling double-hung, energy-efficient windows and, with the police closing in, slaughtered his entire family with a meat cleaver before hanging himself in the closet of the master bedroom.

That was all according to legend, anyway. Like I said, the only death I know for sure happened within these walls is that of Madison Carli Byrd. I know because I was a very big part of it. Bob had quit when he found out we really planned to go through with it. Gemma and I had stripped her naked and held her down on a makeshift altar in the basement while Brian and Jade went at her with knives.

Or at least that had been the plan. With Madison still alive and screaming after at least two dozen slashes, Jade dropped her knife and backed away, causing Brian to stop chanting satanic nonsense and tell her to pick up her knife and stop being a pussy. It was this distraction that had almost caused Madison to escape, but it had been Bernadette, my sweet, four-months-pregnant girlfriend and soon-to-be bride, who had stopped her.

Bernadette tripped Madison to the unfinished floor and climbed on her back, ramming her face against the dirt. In a panic, all of us except Brian, who resumed his ridiculous chanting, tried to stop her.

Finally, we managed to peel Bernadette off of Madison's back, but not before she gouged out our would-be sacrifice's left eye. Blood and a yellow, gelatinous goo spewed from this new wound, and Madison's raw screams became high, infant-like squeals. While the rest of us held Bernadette back, Brian marched forward and rammed the knife into Madison's head, which stopped the piercing cries and reduced her movement to deathly twitching.

We buried her down there, after Brian burned out her eyes (ruined and intact alike) with a cigarette, and swore to never tell a soul, foolishly believing that would somehow keep us safe.

I don't find my son in the Wheeler house, though I search every nook and cranny of the place. I even venture down to the basement, where I unsurprisingly find Madison's grave empty. I'm sure it's been empty for years.

It didn't take long after her execution for the rest of my band to start dying.

First came Gemma's fatal car accident. Her car had gone off the highway and into the path of an oncoming train. Forty-eight hours later, authorities were still finding pieces of her, fused with the remains of her car and scattered across a half-mile stretch of a nearby, wooded state park.

Jade died next. She overdosed on cocaine and heroin. No one could seem to figure out if it was intentional or not. She had spent almost an entire week rotting in some abandoned trailer home before anybody found her.

Brian suffered a vicious attack from his own German Shepherd. The dog had never been aggressive before, and had it not been immediately euthanized, I doubt it would have ever been violent again. Because I don't think it was the dog that did it. Someone or something had used the dog to kill Brian. The same entity that had run Gemma's car off the road, and possessed Jade with the urge to shoot herself with a fatal dose of bad drugs. The same entity that would undoubtedly come for me and Bernadette and our unborn baby.

Only, it didn't, and that was somehow worse. Instead, we

lived with the constant threat that one day it would. Like the sword of Damocles, it hung precariously above our heads, which lay restlessly on one big chopping block.

I was plagued by nightmares of Madison, blacked-out eyes and worm-eaten skin, moving in glitchy spasms as she shuffled toward the bed I shared with my pregnant wife.

Nearly paralyzed with fear for my family's safety, especially after the birth of my son, the usual hyperawareness of life's fragility all the more magnified by Madison's looming presence, I made a deal.

I returned to the Wheeler house. The grave in the basement was already empty by then, but I knew Madison was nearby, so I spoke to her, said I knew she was listening, and sure enough, the house responded with a pulsing green glow that surrounded me, at seemingly random intervals taking the shape of her ruined face.

I told her I'd leave town and take her with me, vowing to tell her story through my songs, as long as she swore to spare my family. She materialized then, kissing me with frostbitten lips and sealing our pact.

After Bernadette went to sleep that night, I took my chilled fifth of Rumple Minze out of the fridge and went into Hunter's room. I spent an hour and a half watching him sleep while I worked my way through the bottle, every gulp burning worse than the one before. After the last swallow of peppermint schnapps, I handwrote a note to Bernadette explaining that I had to leave, that I was sorry, and, though I doubted she'd believe me, I assured her that I was doing this for their protection.

I stuck the note on the refrigerator door with a magnet bearing the Misfits logo, and then I packed up and left.

I drove from Burgundy Woods to Austin, Texas, stopping only once, fully intending to sleep a full night, but mostly ending up just playing guitar with Madison's screams and my baby's cries a maddening duet in my head.

But I held up my end of the deal. My first LP, recorded solo, told Madison's story, in unflinching detail, which is why I don't understand why Hunter is missing. Why did she take him?

I return to Bernadette's house, an empty-handed failure.

I can hardly bring myself to knock, but eventually I raise my hand to do so, and my strike pushes the door open.

And I'm back inside the Wheeler house. Disorientation seizes me, yet I step forward into the dusty darkness, darkness soon lit by that strange green light. Madison's screams and Hunter's infantile cries rise up, not in my head like during that long-ago night in a roadside motel, but all around me. Bernadette's voice joins them, moaning at the peak of her climax. These are the sounds that haunt me most. The sounds I try to drown out with my own trademark wails and a churning wall of distorted guitar and blistering drum. Through every album, save for that first LP that I sometimes think Madison possessed me to write from beyond the grave, I've strived to exorcise these sounds and their accompanying sensations. Hunter's newborn body resting on my chest, his heartbeat a steady pulse against mine. The paralyzing dread I felt as I watched everyone take part in Madison's murder, as her eyeball popped against the pressure of Bernadette's thumb. Bernadette whose cunt was warm, welcoming wetness, the only place I ever really felt safe.

But now it's as if I've taken an extremely high dose of bad drugs, like the one that had killed Jade. As the green light pulses in the darkness, in time with the primal screams, agonized squeals, and ecstatic moans. As Madison and Bernadette emerge from the shadows, fused by the flesh of their torsos, conjoined twins with blacked-out eyes that drag me back to the basement door, my body thumping hard against each stair, back to Madison's empty grave where we all plunge into the cold dirt, a writhing mass of limbs and screams, and after the fall, I look up to see my son standing over us, all grown up and clutching a rusty spade, tears in his eyes, lips quivering, as he begins to cover the grave with dirt, becoming a man with every dig-heave-toss, a man who must bury every bloodstained vestige of his past, lest he endure the punishment for his father's sins.

Hell and Back

Hell for me was a studio apartment in the bad part of town where sirens wailed outside my window, and inside my thoughts were dominated by the wife that left me and the congregation that no longer saw me fit to be their pastor. Where I started drinking again and stopped talking to God. I kept the curtains drawn and slept on the floor.

Inheriting the Deep Well Tavern from my father was my redemption. I started to make my way back from that dark place. I told myself that Hell was a state of mind, that adversity would come, but I would face it on my own terms.

That was all before that night when Danny Carlyle walked into my bar with ghosts in his eyes and a shirt drenched in blood.

Danny was a soft-spoken accountant and a regular at the Deep Well. He was also the only one from my old congregation that still spoke to me. He sat down in front of me, facing his lap where his hands trembled. I put a coaster down and asked if he wanted the usual. He kept his gaze lowered. I said his name.

"Better make it a strong one, Wally," he said.

I gave him my best sympathetic bartender smile and made him a gin and tonic. I told myself that if he got out of control I would flag him, and set the glass on top of the coaster.

Being a bartender is a lot like being a pastor. People confide in you. People expect you to have some cosmos-shifting wisdom to impart, even if deep down you're just as lost as they are.

"Want me to run a tab, Danny?"

He frowned, then reached into his pocket and set a twenty on the bar. "Just take it out of this."

"Hey," I said. "Are you all right?"

He drained his glass and shoved it toward me. "Can you set me up again? Stronger this time, please."

I took the glass but didn't refill it. Instead I stared hard at him.

"What the hell is going on?"

"I killed her."

Without him going into detail, I knew he meant Shelly, his junkie girlfriend. Prone to violent outbursts, she often pushed their confrontations into the physical. I dumped the ice from his glass and called Carrie-Anne over.

"Can you watch the bar for a bit? I need to talk to Danny in the back."

"Sure, Wally."

I hoped the noises from the other conversations had drowned out Danny's confession. I stepped around the other side of the bar and took him by the elbow. We walked through the kitchen and into my office.

"Have a seat," I said.

He collapsed into the chair. His haunted eyes reminded me that I hadn't misheard him. Danny Carlyle, man of faith, soft-spoken accountant and regular at my bar, was a murderer.

"Now," I said, "I want you to start from the beginning. Tell me exactly what happened."

"I came home tonight. She'd been clean for a while." He pulled a pack of cigarettes from his jacket pocket. I didn't remember him being a smoker and I almost told him not to smoke in my office, but considering his plight, I let him pass. "I actually caught her stealing something from me so she could go out and get a fix. We started fighting. I tried to restrain her and she took a knife from the kitchen. I tried to disarm her, but in the struggle...God..."

He sucked on the cigarette and blew smoke around the room. He unzipped his jacket and revealed his blood-soaked shirt. Danny stood and opened his jacket all the way.

"My God, Wally, I killed the woman I love." He got on his knees before me, tears falling from his haunted eyes, and took my hand into an iron grip. It was like the old days, when I made the altar call and folks came up to accept Christ and ask for forgiveness. Sometimes they meant it; other times I knew they were full of shit. "Wally, I don't know what to do, man. You gotta help me."

His plea resonated. I said, "Why not try the police? Why'd you come here?"

"The police? They will..."

"If it was self-defense..."

"It was! But this would ruin me. I will lose my job. I'll lose everything, even if my name is cleared."

He was right. He was a good man, but the public wouldn't see it that way. His employer wouldn't. His ex-wife wouldn't, and she would make sure he never saw his kids again. All they would see is a man who kept company with drug addicts half his age. I pried his hands off of mine, then placed my hands on his shoulders.

"Take me to her," I said.

Shelley was lying on the floor of Danny's house, her cold, lifeless eyes looking at me as I stood in the doorway. The handle of the knife jutted out of her chest. Blood pooled in the carpet around her. He got her in the heart. Sickness rose within me at the sight of her and I held my hand to my mouth and gagged.

Danny went to the couch and picked up a cell phone. A grim expression crossed his face and he appeared more angry than scared. He set the phone back down.

"Close the door, please," he said.

As I stood in his living room, I wondered over and over why I agreed to come with him. I shut the door behind me.

"I thought we might, uh, roll her up in that carpet." He sniffed. "My back seats go down. We could dump her somewhere."

I fought the urge to turn and run out the door. To rat out my friend. I reminded myself that he needed my help, that this was the only real option. Even if there was more to this, he'd seen fit to forgive me. I should offer him the same absolution. I swallowed.

"Let's get this over with. Do you have a box cutter? We have to get this carpet up."

He nodded and went to the other room. I knelt beside Shelly's head and stared deep into her dead eyes. It's *all right*, I told myself. From what I knew about her, no one would come looking.

Danny only owned one box cutter, so I cut the carpet for him. I sent him to the kitchen to make himself a drink. God knew he needed it. Me, I needed to stay sharp and sober, if I was going to get my friend out of this. I felt bad for him and wanted to make sure I did everything I could to help. Besides, now if I fucked up, it was my ass, too.

I started to turn a corner with the blade when the phone on the couch rang again. Danny jumped out of his seat, checked the screen, and silenced the ringing.

"Who is it?" I asked.

"Nobody."

"Is that her phone? We can't have someone come looking for her, man."

"I said it was nobody."

I grimaced and resumed cutting the carpet. The tearing sound soothed me, so I focused on it, tried to tell myself we would finish soon. The phone rang again. He trembled and silenced it. I glared at him, but he ignored me. Before I resumed cutting, the phone beeped twice, a text message. Danny glanced at it.

"Shit," he said. "Can't you go any faster?"

I stood. "Danny, what the hell aren't you telling me?"

"Nothing, we just…"

"Who keeps calling?"

"Wally…"

I snatched the phone from his hand. The text was from someone named Ryan.

WHAT'S GOING ON, WHY AREN'T YOU ANSWERING YOUR PHONE? it read

"Who's Ryan?"

"Just forget it, Wally. We got to finish this."

"You're asking me to be an accessory to murder; I suggest you give me as much information as possible."

The phone went off again.

I showed Danny the message: I'M COMING OVER THERE. "Ryan's her other boyfriend," Danny said. "He gets her drugs; she gives him her body." He paused and dropped his gaze. "She was gonna leave me for him."

"Son of a bitch," I said. He didn't need to say anything else. "You handle this. I can't be a part..."

"But you already are. Your fingerprints are all over everything. You were seen leaving the bar with me. Listen, when they caught your hand in the collection plate, and your wife left you, and the elders fired you, I stuck by you. I stuck by you because I knew you were just like me."

My jaw clenched.

"Now," he said, "let's get this done before Ryan gets here."

I got back on my knees. I couldn't cut fast enough. The entire time I couldn't shake the notion I was fucked. Part of me wanted to take the box cutter and ram it into Danny's throat.

I finished cutting and retracted the blade. "Back up your car, Danny."

He nodded and got to his feet. I cursed as he passed by. My blood boiled in my veins as I knelt looking into Shelley's eyes. They hypnotized me, sending my thoughts to the dark place.

I remembered the day I got the news. The elders in my congregation sat me down in my office and told me I was unfit to lead a congregation. If I couldn't manage a family, how could I attend to the spiritual needs of a community?

There were nights the feelings of betrayal got so strong, I wanted to kill my ex-wife for ruining me. Recalling this, I recognized a kindred spirit in Danny. We both possessed this darkness within us. Danny was my brother. I could forgive him, even if no one would forgive me.

The car started and I silently urged him to hurry.

After he backed the car up to the front door, I came outside and opened the trunk. He put the seats down and I gave him a nod. We went back inside and began rolling her up in the carpet.

Danny extracted the knife with a squishing sound. It took everything not to vomit as blood bubbled from the wound. With the knife removed, I took one side of the carpet and covered her with it. Danny folded the other end over.

"You have duct tape?"

He nodded and started to get up.

"I'll get it. You hold her together. Where is it?"

He pointed toward a drawer in the kitchen and I went. I opened every drawer until I found it, then went back to the living room. My pulse pounded as time ran out. What would the wage of our sin be?

"Lift her," I said, pulling a length of tape free.

He did and I wrapped one end of the carpet tightly in tape. I did the same around the opposite end and put several pieces of tape across the middle. Our eyes met and I nodded. We each took an end, I counted to three, and we lifted. My muscles strained; death had a way of making a body heavy. We exited into the night and I prayed that the darkness would be sufficient to cover our deed. In the distance, an approaching engine whined. I met eyes with Danny and his expression matched what I felt.

"We have to hurry."

I quickened my pace as we approached the trunk. When we reached it, I rested her head and shoulders on the edge of the car. We repositioned ourselves to the sides of her body like two pallbearers carrying a coffin.

The whine of the engine got closer. I had to go around and get her over a bump near the seats. I pulled. The car turned down Danny's street.

"Shit," Danny said. "Shit, shit, shit!"

She was in all the way.

"Danny, shut the trunk!"

The car's brakes screeched to a halt in front of Danny's house. Danny shut the trunk and I closed the back door. We exchanged glances. Panic filled Danny's eyes.

The driver got out, and I turned to face him.

Ryan wore a sports jersey and baggy jeans. The brim of a baseball cap partially hid his youthful features. Mostly skin and bone, the baggy clothes made him appear bigger.

"What the fuck is this?" he said. He lifted his shirt to reveal the grip of a Glock. "Where's Shelley?"

He came closer.

"You're Ryan?" Danny stepped forward, probably not seeing the gun. "You just mind your damn business, you little…"

"Wait," I stepped in Danny's way, "let's just all…"

"What the fuck? Is that blood?" Ryan pointed at Danny's shirt.

I followed the gesture to the mess of red splattered on Danny's chest. Ryan pulled the gun.

"Where's Shelley?" He shifted his aim from Danny to me. "What the hell did you guys do to her?"

A door opened.

"What did you guys do to Shelley?"

I froze as the neighbor stepped out of their home to investigate the commotion. Whether Ryan shot me or not, I was fucked. No two ways about it. More people appeared outside as Ryan kept screaming at us. He pointed the gun back and forth.

"You sons of bitches, what have you done? What have you done?" Tears glistened in his eyes. For all I knew, he and Shelley had planned on getting clean. Skipping town. Getting married. "What have you…?"

"You shut the fuck up!" Danny came forward, pointing a finger at Ryan as if he, too, held a gun. "One thing I'm not gonna do is be scared by some two-bit drug dealer with a gun."

"Danny…" I said.

"You stay where you are, old man!" Ryan kept the gun trained on Danny.

Danny didn't stop advancing toward Ryan. "I'll choke the miserable life out of you, little punk. I…"

Ryan fired. Chunks of brain sprayed from the back of Danny's head. Ryan stared at the weapon and threw it. He took his hat off and stared across the lawn at me.

Someone had called the police and their sirens wailed in the night. Ryan paced while I stood still. We both knew what was coming. Neither of us would get out of this. Too many people saw us and our cars. Some went back into their houses, but watched from behind their windows.

Ryan threw his hands up and got back in his car. He fired up the engine and sped away. His tail lights disappeared into the night. They would catch him. Poor kid. Before this he'd been a fuck-up, not a killer. I went back into the house, the acceptance of my arrest coming easier than I thought it would. I found a blanket and went back outside to cover Danny with it. I wanted to give the poor bastard some dignity.

As the first of the police cars pulled onto the street, I stepped off the lawn and onto the pavement. Spotlighted in red and blue, I put my hands on my head and got down on my knees to beg for mercy.

Our Lady of the Sea

Harrison didn't see the gray-skinned little girl limping down the sidewalk until the third night in Douglas's shore house.

He deleted all his social media accounts. Quit his day job. Changed his phone number. His therapist said he was isolating. He told her she was probably right, but he wasn't changing his mind.

"Are you thinking about hurting yourself?" she asked.

"Don't be ridiculous."

That appeased her curiosity, but it was a lie. He was considering the option of suicide, but Douglas had given him the shore house, and Harrison promised he'd try to sort things out, and if he couldn't, he wouldn't kill himself in Douglas's house. At the very least, Harrison would walk into the ocean until the water drifted over his head. He'd never been much of a swimmer. He hated guns and the idea of cutting himself open made him queasy. Hanging and overdosing left too much room for error. He'd drown himself in the ocean.

That appeased Douglas. He didn't believe Harrison would actually do it. He'd known Harrison for too long and thought Harrison was full of shit.

The girl wasn't a zombie. One, zombies weren't real. Two, she wasn't solid enough. There's nothing like Ocean City during the winter, especially during a blizzard. Except for the girl, the streets were empty. Most of the businesses and shore homes were closed. During the day, he could hear church bells, but right now the silence was absolute. The snow drifts blew through her. He was sure of it. Some of the flakes got stuck inside and danced underneath her ethereal skin before floating outside her body.

She's a ghost, then, which didn't seem so ridiculous. He'd always believed in ghosts, though he'd never actually seen one. He wanted to see her up close, to find out her name, to find out what happened to her, to find out why she stayed behind.

He was wearing sweats to stay warm while he slept. He left those on and pulled his winter coat and snow boots on over top of them. He grabbed the keys to Douglas's house, and, as an afterthought, his notebook. He'd gotten better about bringing his notebook with him places. Helped him jot down ideas so he didn't forget them by the time he sat down at his laptop.

He descended the stairs and stepped out into the snowy night. She was walking away from him. More like levitating. Her feet, less than six inches above the ground, left no impressions. She was headed toward the sea.

He trudged through the snow after her. He'd always wanted to meet a ghost. Since she didn't have to contend with the knee-deep snow, she outpaced him. He lunged forward, tried to quicken his pace, and he fell face-forward. The snow stung against his face, choked his breath and muffled his hearing. It's like he imagined drowning. The snow had a clean smell and he toyed with the idea of staying underneath with his head down, wondered how long it would take to die of hypothermia.

But he wasn't ready. Not sure he'd ever be ready. And he forced himself to his feet.

The girl was gone.

He tried to make a list of reasons to stay alive a week before coming to Douglas's shore house. For every reason he came up with, he had a counter-reason.

His soon to be ex-wife. Hated him.

The unborn son in her womb. Would be better off not knowing him.

His mistress. Hated him.

His career. More of a pain in the ass now than the rewarding endeavor it used to be.

His therapist. She'd get over it.

Douglas. Well, he was a decent guy, always been there in the past, and now here he was letting Harrison stay at his house to sort things out. He deserved better as a best friend.

The only reason Harrison wasn't dead was he made an agreement with himself. He would at least try. He would strip everything away. Isolate himself so he could sort things out. Find a real reason to live. Find out if he wanted to live for *himself* and no one else. Find out if he could.

Douglas said to take as much time as he needed, but Harrison gave himself two weeks.

Two weeks should be enough.

Two weeks to decide if he wanted to live or die.

The first night in Douglas's house passed without him getting any sleep. He slept a little on the second night, but not nearly enough.

Now, after seeing the ghost, he knew he wouldn't do much sleeping the third night either. Instead he showered, doing his damnedest to get warm, but the water wouldn't get quite hot enough. All the time he was under its spray, he closed his eyes and pictured the girl floating above the snow, but limping like she was walking and in pain, her gray skin translucent.

He wondered what it'd be like to hold her hand, to help her cross over. Maybe the two of them could cross over together. He could walk with her to the water's edge and cradle her in his arms and walk into the sea. She could be his strength and he could be hers.

He turned his face up to the showerhead and knelt beneath the flow. He was practicing, he told himself, as the water dripped down his cheeks, into his eyes, over his nose and lips. He ended the death rehearsal when his phone rang.

"Douglas, what's up?"

"Hey. I know I said I wouldn't call, but I just…guess I'm worried."

Douglas's voice always reminded him of a teacher he had in the fourth grade. A man who insisted the class call him Mr. T. because his Japanese last name was too difficult for ten-year-olds to pronounce. Soft-spoken, he delivered every sentence with a smile you could hear. He attributed this to his background in sales.

"Are you there?" Douglas asked.

"I'm here. Just got out of the shower."

"Well, at least you're taking care of yourself."

"I guess. Not doing much sleeping."

"That's not good…"

"Yeah, listen, you ever see a…" He stopped yourself. How should he finish that sentence? *You ever see a little girl around here?* Given that Douglas only stayed here in the summer, he'd probably seen lots of little girls. *You ever see any ghosts?* Yeah, he didn't need Douglas thinking the lack of sleep was making him see ghosts. As far as he knew, Douglas was a man of science with no belief in the supernatural. "You ever see a blizzard out here? It's beautiful."

He went to the window to watch the snow fall, to watch for the girl. But he didn't see her.

"It never snows in the summer. I was here in six years ago to clean up after Hurricane Darla though. All that sand looked like snow in the right light."

Harrison didn't laugh. He closed the curtains and sat on the edge of the bed.

"Well, if you're okay…"

"Fine," Harrison said, too snappy.

Douglas sighed on the other end. "I guess I'll let you go. Be sure to call if you need anything."

"Will do."

Harrison disconnected.

When the nail heads protruding from the walls started to bleed, he thought it was rust until he got a closer look. The liquid was a too-deep shade of red. It was blood, but he couldn't begin to imagine why. He could only watch it drip and stain the wall with crimson tears. He was mesmerized. Fascinated. Queasiness broke his hypnosis and he almost vomited.

He ran to the bathroom, wet a towel, and returned to scrub the walls clean…but they were already clean. It was as if no blood had just been oozing through the wallpaper around the nail heads. Harrison stood there, towel clutched in his fist, trying to make sense of what he saw.

It was his fourth night in Douglas's house. The sleep he got on the second night was the only sleep he'd gotten so far.

He blinked, expecting the blood to reappear. He perked his ears, listening for...for what? Something in the walls?

He ran to the window, expecting to see the girl. The snow had stopped, but no one had plowed it. He stared at the street submerged in white. His tired reflection caught his eye. He imagined his skin gray and translucent, the light from the desk lamp passing through it. He didn't see the girl anywhere and his vision blurred. His eyes stung.

He was crying.

The next day, the roads had been plowed, the sidewalks shoveled. Harrison treated himself to a walk. Everything was quiet and closed down, but he heard the church bells and walked in the direction he thought they were coming from.

The church was white-walled, adobe-like, the cross rising from the steeple, the same color of the church walls and made of the same material. The stained glass windows were darkened. The bells were stopped, bent at angles to give the illusion of movement, but the ringing was coming from a loudspeaker positioned underneath. A broad-shouldered man with thinning brown hair and a pot belly stopped shoveling snow and turned to look at Harrison. His eyes squinted behind his glasses and he smiled.

Harrison had never been religious, but he'd always liked preachers. He liked people who got fired up about something, even if that something was a man in the sky who didn't like it when he touched himself. Harrison waved. The preacher stepped forward, extended his hand. They shook.

"Reverend Isaiah Gorman," he said.

"Harrison."

"Haven't seen you around here before," he said.

"Bet you don't see much of anyone during the winter."

"If I were a betting man I wouldn't bet against you. What brings you out here this time of year?"

"I needed some quiet. Thought the shore during the winter was a safe bet."

"Again, I wouldn't bet against you." He grinned big. His teeth were yellow, but straight. "Some of the old folks stay all year round. Most of them make up my congregation. Are you a churchgoing man?"

Harrison cocked his head to the side, tried to smile back. "Hey, we just met. No religion or politics, okay?"

"Our Lady is bigger than any religion."

"Your Lady?"

"Why, yes." He glanced up at the cross. His laugh was like sandpaper on tree bark. "What? You thought I was going to ask if you'd met my friend Jesus?"

"Yeah, guess I kind of did. So, what religion is this?"

"The only one that matters around here," he said. "You'll have to join us sometime."

"Maybe I will," Harrison said, knowing full well he wouldn't.

"She's been good to us since the storm."

"Not so good then, huh?" Harrison laughed. The preacher didn't.

"Our Lady may do with us as she pleases. When in our pride we forget her we get our comeuppance."

Harrison shook Gorman's hand again. Harrison liked him, even though he was probably crazy. He didn't have that crazy look though. Harrison had had his fair share of run-ins with emotionally disturbed vagrants during his time living in Philly. Many of them had the same darting glance, clothes in disrepair, hair unkempt.

Harrison broke the handshake and made another false promise of turning up at the next service. He walked away. The bells droned through the static of the loud speaker. The tinny sound tickled his skin with tiny electric fingers.

The four hours of sleep he got was solid, dreamless. He woke feeling refreshed. He even cooked for himself instead of munching on granola bars. After a breakfast of a spinach omelet, he got some writing done. The ten handwritten pages felt good, like a return to form after damn near a year of failed attempts at other genres, other voices, even other mediums. He didn't think about suicide at all.

He napped in the afternoon and when he woke, it was dark again. He made himself pasta with red sauce and wrote three more pages. A line into the fourth page, the church bells started to chime. He glanced at the bedside clock. It was nine-thirty. What the hell was going on in the church at nine-thirty?

He went to the window and saw the girl. Her motions gave the illusion of limping, but he was sure she was levitating again. He didn't bother to put on his boots and coat. He ran downstairs and out the front door. Catching up to her was the most important thing he could ever do. He stopped and gazed in her direction.

The girl was at least twenty paces ahead and headed for the church.

"Hey," he said. "Wait up."

She ignored him. He started walking fast. He kept calling out. She crossed the main drag and he followed, jaywalking as the light turned red. No matter how fast he went, she remained twenty paces ahead. Even as she retained the same speed.

The girl approached the church entrance. The door opened without her touching it. She drifted through and the door closed behind her. He broke into a run, almost face-planted in the gutter across from the church, righted himself and trotted up the salted church steps. The bells were drowned out by the sound of an organ, but the tune was unlike any church song he'd ever heard. The organist was leaning on a chord, sounding like he or she was grinding their fingers into the keys. It was minor. Diminished. Weird. His stomach sank. His mouth went dry.

He pushed open the door to the church. Reverend Gorman stood at the pulpit, petting the head of a lamb. Behind him was a mural depicting a nude woman levitating above a sea of roiling waves. The organist had stringy black hair that covered their face. Every few seconds their shoulders rolled forward as pressure was reapplied to the chord. The pews were full of the old and decrepit. Wrinkled eyes agog. Lizard lips hung open, leaking drool.

The girl was nowhere to be found. Harrison looked over

his shoulder, thought about running outside, but the reverend's voice concussed the PA system and Harrison froze.

"Our Lady of the Sea," he said. "You've rained a generous bounty upon us in the time since the flood, in the years since we turned back to you in fear and love. Look upon us, your lonely congregation. Have pity and look with favor on our sacrifice."

Harrison turned back to the altar. He had to see for himself, even though he knew damn well blood would be spilled.

Gorman pulled a curved dagger from his vestments.

"Find favor with us, O Lady," he said.

He dragged the blade across the lamb's throat. Blood dyed the wool red. The lamb jerked its head side to side, gagging as it screamed. Gorman's eyes rolled back in ecstasy. He raised the blade. Looked to the heavens. The mural of waves began to move. The nude woman smiled.

Gorman lowered his head. Darkness filled his eyes and those eyes zeroed in on Harrison. Harrison expected him to point and howl like Donald Sutherland in that Body Snatchers movie. Even though he didn't, the rest of the congregation turned around to stare. The lamb plopped to the ground, jerking in its death throes. Harrison backed out the door, never taking his eyes from the reverend and his followers. He was afraid that if he looked away for as much as a second, they'd find a way to move in on him and drag him to the altar to be the next sacrifice.

When he got through the door and it closed without anyone advancing on him, Harrison turned and ran back to Douglas's house. He locked himself in, drew all the curtains, and kept the lights off. Shivering from cold and fright, he crawled up the stairs and felt around for his phone. When he found it, he dialed Douglas.

The line rang once. There was a playback of church bells. He stared at the faceplate, made sure he dialed the right number. The bells continued, crackling through the phone's earpiece until they were drowned out by the gurgling cry of a lamb with its throat slit.

He hung up. 9-1-1 gave him the same damned bells. He threw the phone against the wall. The church bells didn't stop. They echoed up and down the street.

He paced the room in the dark, telling himself he wasn't going crazy, that he really saw what he saw and that was somehow worse. He was tired and crawled into bed, put his face under the pillow and screamed until his throat went raw and exhaustion pulled him under.

He woke up feeling hungover even though he hadn't had a drink in almost a year. He groaned. His limbs felt like they were full of bricks. The scene from the church came back to him. In the daylight, it almost seemed silly, but he *knew* he didn't dream it. He really followed the ghost to the church. Reverend Gorman really slit the throat of a lamb. The mural depicting the lady of the sea really moved.

His head spun. He felt sick. An attempt at vomiting in the toilet yielded painful dry heaves.

He re-entered the bedroom and picked his phone up off the ground. Its protective case was scuffed, but otherwise the device was intact. He dialed Douglas's number.

"Harrison," Douglas answered.

A lump closed Harrison's throat. He had no idea what he was going to say. He searched his thoughts. Douglas said his name again. This time he sounded worried. Almost panicked.

"Hey, Douglas, do you know anything about Reverend Gorman?"

He laughed. "Oh yeah. Our Lady of the Sea. What about him?"

"What do you know about his church?"

"I don't know. It opened the summer after Darla. There was a big controversy because him and his congregation used to be Pentecostals, even used the same building they use now. It was in the papers and everything. Surprised you didn't hear about it."

Harrison tried to remember. Sort of recalled something about a Christian church converting to a pagan religion.

"Hey, listen," Harrison said, "have any kids gone missing around here that you know about?"

"What's this about?" Douglas asked.

"I don't know. I'm not sure yet."

His gaze drifted to the protruding nail heads. Blood darkened the surrounding drywall. Three red spots the size of quarters.

"Douglas, I'll call you back."

He hung up and ran to the wall. He daubed one of the spots with his finger and sniffed the coppery fluid. Definitely blood.

He ran to the bathroom and wet a towel. This time the blood didn't disappear. He scrubbed the fresh blood away, but couldn't remove the stains. He glanced from the wall to the towel. Each movement of his head accented the downbeat of his heart's frantic rhythm.

Something thumped behind the wall. He jolted. He dropped the towel, put his ear to the wall and listened. Another thump. He got up and ran downstairs. He rummaged through the house until he found what he was looking for and scrambled back upstairs.

He raised the hammer to strike the wall, waited to hear another thump. Nothing. He grew impatient.

"If you're back there, just get as far away from the wall as possible. I'll get you out of there."

He had no idea what to expect. Maybe the girl. Or another child. Or maybe just an animal. A cat. A rat. He struck the wall. Once, twice, three times. The plaster started to give. He swung with more ferocity, obsessed, as if what lay behind the wall was the most important piece of the puzzle, vital to helping him sort things out. Blood leaked from the edge of the hole. He kept striking. He dropped the hammer and started to kick, widening the hole. Cold blood spattered his bare foot, but he didn't stop.

With the hole as wide as a watermelon, he reached through, felt something like matted cotton. He tugged at something heavy and groaned as he strained. He got part of it through the wall and fell backward.

Blinking, his tailbone throbbing, he tried to regain his composure. The lamb's head lolled out of the hole in the wall, dead eyes staring, a crimson smile-shaped wound on its neck. He called 9-1-1 and this time someone answered and he gave them the address.

"Yes, I need police. I found a..." he transfixed his gaze to the slaughtered lamb, "a dead animal in my wall…a lamb…no, I don't know how it got there…its throat was slit…yes, I'll be here. Thanks."

He thought maybe he should tell them what he saw at the church, but decided they wouldn't believe him. He sat on the bed, staring down the slaughtered animal, and waited for the police to arrive.

Half an hour passed before officers came. Harrison went downstairs to greet them. The one in front was a short and dark-haired man with a young face. Behind him stood a tall blond with a buzz cut and wrinkles around sky-blue eyes. Concern marked their expressions and Harrison realized they thought he was ninety-six. He knew that ten code from a ride-along he did while researching his first book. Ninety-six meant emotionally disturbed person. In less politically correct terms, batshit crazy.

That's okay, he thought. *They'll see the lamb for themselves. They'll have no choice but to believe me.*

The short, dark-haired cop made small talk. Asked what Harrison was doing down the shore in the winter. Asked what Harrison did for work. Asked if Harrison was here alone.

Harrison told him he was staying somewhere quiet so he could finish his next book, and yes, he was here alone.

The officers followed him inside and upstairs to the bedroom. Dust and shards of drywall littered the floor. The ragged hole gaped, but there was no lamb, no blood. One of the officers sighed. Harrison balled his hands into fists. They patronized him long enough to decide that he wasn't going to harm himself or anyone else, and left him to collapse back on the bed, wondering if he really was emotionally disturbed, batshit crazy.

He grabbed his notebook and flipped it open. His scrawl filled the first thirteen pages, but not the words he remembered writing the other night. Though he recalled writing a ghost story, about a group of road-trippers who cross paths with an undead girl who walks the streets of an abandoned town, the pages were filled with one line repeated over and over.

I'm going under, under, under. Going under, under, under.

He flipped through the pages, reading and re-reading. He shook his head, as trying to make sense of it physically hurt. The bells rang through the streets again. He cried out and threw the notebook across the room.

He scrambled downstairs, not sure what he was doing or why. The bells clanged over and over, their rhythm irregular, their tone dissonant. He entered the kitchen and grabbed a knife with a thick dull blade. He pushed out the front door, drool soaking his chin before freezing in the wind. He glanced back and forth, feeling rabid. He just wanted to stab things. Not himself, he was still lucid enough for that idea to make him nauseous, but he told himself he'd stab anything that got too close. No reason, just boiling rage. *Maybe you can cut through the madness, release yourself from this nightmare.*

And he saw her. She was walking away from the church. Coming toward him. Her feet drifted mere inches from the frosted ground. The buildings behind her were visible through her gray skin. He clutched the knife in both hands, bracing against the chilling wind, against the urge to lunge forward, against the urge to scream.

She came closer. Something was growling. It was him.

The closer she got the warmer he felt. It was the opposite of everything he'd heard about ghosts. It was like standing next to a fire, a fire that was spreading, its flames drawing nearer to his skin.

He coughed, started to laugh. His skin was burning. The girl was getting closer, arm's length. His hands trembled, dropped the knife. She was kissing distance. His flesh sizzled. She embraced him. His laughs became screams.

He woke on the beach, knees planted in a wet mix of snow and sand, something heavy resting in his lap. The bells hadn't stopped. He smelled salt water, kelp, and something rotting. He was soaked, freezing. Slushy drops fell from his hair, streamed down his face. The waves crested and exploded against the shore. The tide was coming in. It was almost night. Darkness clouded the sky across the sea.

"O dear Lady." It was Gorman, somewhere behind Harrison.

Other voices joined his, speaking in tongues. The voices were rapturous, but cracked with age and decay. A wave crashed. Closer now. A fine mist blew across Harrison's face.

He looked down at the heavy thing in his lap. The dead lamb stared back, tongue lolling, neck twisted at an unnatural angle. It was near full dark now and Harrison was paralyzed.

Not a star was visible. Blackness swallowed everything, but he was awake, present for it. The voices continued to chant. The bells continued to ring. Gorman wept tears of joy. The waves drew closer. A light rose from them. Blue in color. A halo of ethereal tentacles surrounded its nucleus.

Harrison couldn't speak or scream. Couldn't get up to run or even shake the lamb's corpse from his lap. The light took the form of a woman, levitating above the black waves, waves that spilled closer, soaking his knees and shins.

It was the woman from the church. The one in the mural. Our Lady of the Sea. At her feet knelt a child, the gray-skinned girl. Only now she was blue and weeping.

Harrison remembered his plan. If he couldn't sort things out by the end of the two weeks, he'd walk into the ocean until the water came over his head. He'd drown himself. But here he was, only five days into his stay, the sea about to wash over him, but damn it all, he wanted to live. He so badly needed to live, to see what was next, to try and repair the schisms between himself and his loved ones.

But he couldn't even move. He couldn't even scream as the Lady of the Sea wrapped him in her cold, black embrace.

Worlds Colliding

DOMINIC

Ever meet someone and feel like it's fate? I'm sure. For the woman at the bar staring down a vodka tonic. The co-worker who signs all his emails with: "For God So Loved the World." The lady who walks the one-eyed Pit Bull. The universe will bond you to them. Make you inseparable even in the most terrible circumstances.

Here's the thing: it's all bullshit.

You are drawn to these people, not by the machines of destiny or by some deity who moves people around in a calculated, deliberate way, but by a force within you. It craves a certain type of energy. Senses the potential for collision. Pushes you forward until you can no longer avoid it.

Sometimes, one quick but devastating crash leaves you maimed beyond repair. Other times, a series of crashes over a prolonged period. You try to swerve out of the way, or you think you do, but you're just allowing yourself a brief respite so you can catch your breath before the next encounter.

What's awful about these sorts of relationships is you know they're bad for you. They will only bring pain. Every time you get away, you'll circle back one day.

The same energy dwelt within her and pushed her toward me. I say this, because she initiated contact. She suggested we get together outside of work.

I went to her house and we drank rum and talked about bands we liked. She had downgraded from Captain Morgan to some bottom-shelf brand that tasted like rubbing alcohol and chili powder. It didn't seem to bother her in the least. She sipped the shit straight, without as much as a grimace. She caught on to my apprehension and offered me a can of Coke to use as a chaser. Even with the soda, the booze went down hard.

She told me even though she seemed happy and bright, she had a dark side. I just smiled and told her it was okay. We are all complex creatures. Some New Age crap like that.

I used to think I wanted to fix people, that some noble, chivalrous spirit propelled my every action.

I learned otherwise a long time ago. I just like to watch shit burn.

Once we went out for karaoke. I sang better than ever that night. Something about being in the midst of chaotic forces brings out the artist in me. I performed that song from Airborne Toxic Event and on that line about seeing ghosts, I screamed from somewhere deep.

I cried out because so far she and I only experienced fender benders. No twisted metal. No total losses. No fatalities on the road.

But I needed the blood, the ravaged limbs, the injuries I would live with for the rest of my life.

We almost got our crash.

We stayed out too late. Around one in the morning, her husband called. Asked where we were and what we were we doing. I told him we'd be back soon.

I hung up with him. Asked Nora if he'd get rough with her.

She shrugged off my question, smiled and said, "I'll just offer him sex. That will cool him off."

Or you could just screw me and we could drive the hell out of here and never look back, I thought, but didn't say. Fucked up, yeah, but I was ready for blood and fire.

When it came time to part ways, I hugged her and told her to be careful. She told me she had it under control and staggered out of my car up to the front door.

I drove home with the windows down. Gushes of cold air made my eyes bleed water.

NORA

I used to think I wanted to be near him because he was strong, but the longer our friendship lasted, I find that's not true. He surrounds himself with people who he perceives to be falling apart. When around people better than him, he withers. It's not his strength that draws me to him, but his weakness. His weakness for me allows him to smile when I show him my scars. Forbids him to cry over my fresh wounds until he's somewhere he thinks I can't see him.

He's nothing like Brian. He never tells me I'm a fool for hurting myself, for getting drunk into oblivion, for wanting to die. He's so fucking diplomatic. *It hurts to see you hurt, but I can't stop you. I'd miss you if you were gone.*

Every time we meet, I weigh my options. Do I show how much it sucks to exist? Or do I smile and pretend I overcame somehow? Tell him I'm happy. Tell him I'm sober. Tell him Brian and I are no longer fighting.

He sat across from me at the diner, eyes dark and sunken like he hadn't slept for days, hair unkempt and beard stubble growing in (he normally was so clean cut), and clutching his coffee cup as if only its warmth kept him alive.

"I'm in love," he said.

I think he may be in danger.

When he dropped me off, I put my hand on his arm.

"Don't go," I said.

He looked down at my hand, eyes widened. He met my gaze and we kissed. Years of untapped desire broke loose and in a matter of seconds I was fucking him in his car, not giving a damn at any moment my husband could come outside. I ground against his cock, held my arm to his mouth and forced him to lick my scars.

He screamed when he came and cried afterward.

I went inside, kissed Brian on my way to the bathroom, and sat on the toilet where I smoked and pissed his seed out of me.

I don't even think it was the sex. I think it was the scars.

Letting him kiss them embodied his total devotion to me and mine to him. Didn't matter I was married or he was in love. We belonged to each other now. Nothing could take that away.

DOMINIC

She came to the wedding and brought her husband. Somehow that didn't end in disaster.

I seldom thought of her as I settled into married life, tried to enjoy every moment of the honeymoon phase. You would think when you're used to things falling apart, you would be better able to appreciate when things are going well. Like the idea about being pushed around by invisible hands of fate, that's simply not true. Every day is spent in fear, because deep down you know one day the bottom is going to give way and leave you to fall spiraling into the black infinite.

She called me and said Brian hit her. I couldn't believe he never struck her before.

"Do you want me to come get you?" I asked.

"Could you?"

I told Claire what happened and she agreed to let me bring Nora to our place. Claire's a good soul. I'm not sure what she sees in me. If Claire has the same attraction to chaos I do, I have yet to see it. Her ex-husband lost his legs in an accident and later committed suicide, but she finished grieving over him before she met me.

The three of us got high and Claire cooked dinner. We watched some psychedelic science fiction film from the 1970s with the sound turned down and listened to dubstep in the background. Everything was fine, just three friends hanging out, until Nora started getting sloppy: a lot of crying, a lot of nodding off and complaining of nausea. She stumbled off to the bathroom and turned on the shower.

"We could go inside and molest her," I said.

"That's not funny."

I shrugged. I went to the door.

"Hey, you okay in there?"

Nothing.

I waited almost a minute, knocked. She didn't respond. I turned to Claire.

"She's fine," she said.

"I don't know."

"Don't worry about her. It's a cry for attention. If you stop banging on the door, I give her two minutes before she comes out."

I searched my thoughts and found I agreed.

When Nora finally came out I walked her to my car and drove her home.

"I'm glad it's over," she said. "He only cares about himself. He never fucking listens to me and doesn't get me."

Her words sounded scripted, but I didn't doubt their veracity.

"I'm sorry," I said, not sure why I said it. Sometimes it seems like the only right thing to say.

We drove, another collision inevitable, a real blood-and-glass-on-the-highway wreck.

"It's hard when you don't feel anything for someone," she said, and I wonder why she married him. "I'm not attracted to him."

Again, I wondered about her process when she first met him. Why didn't she stop the train before it derailed? I answered my own question: she craved the crash as much as I did. A reckless driver, she swerved from lane to lane, driving up on the sidewalk and clipping pedestrians, slamming on her brakes in the middle of a high-speed thoroughfare. A disaster on wheels and I wanted along for the ride.

"Call me if you need anything," I said.

"I will. Thank you."

I stopped myself from reaching for her and she left my car without another word.

I came home to a dark house and a sleeping Claire.

"Hey," I said. "Well, that was fun."

She groaned.

"I'm sorry she got so crazy."

My wife stayed quiet for a long time. I thought she had fallen back asleep. I lay down beside her and she spoke up, startling me.

"Be careful with her," she said. "Sometimes people do rash things to get attention."

"Yeah, true."

"She left her underwear in our bathroom."

"What?"

"You heard me."

"Well, that's weird."

"Not really. She probably hoped you would find them."

"Maybe she was just wasted."

"Maybe."

I stayed awake in the darkness and didn't say another word.

NORA

I imagined Dominic finding those panties. Pictured him stashing them somewhere until a time his wife wasn't home. Wrapping them around his shaft and stroking himself to orgasm. Milky rivulets of semen spilling down their silk crotch.

Only he never mentioned them to me. Claire didn't either, thankfully. A week passed without contact. I ignored calls from my husband, drank rum, and cried often. Mostly I just sat in the dark; the only honest thing to do, sometimes even comforted me enough so I could drift off to sleep. Sleep forever. Sink into perfect darkness, never dreaming, never waking again.

Thinking of this gave me an idea. I took out my phone and started texting him song lyrics from Marilyn Manson's *Eat Me, Drink Me*. The breakup album. No one seemed to care when it came out, but Dominic and I shared an appreciation for it. The LP is flawed in a way only a person in the worst place in their life could make.

He texted me back. I LOVE THAT SONG. HOW ARE YOU DOING?

My response: KIND OF HOW I FEEL RIGHT NOW. EVERYTHING BURNED DOWN. EIGHT YEARS OF MARRIAGE.

I CAN'T EVEN PRETEND TO KNOW WHAT THAT'S LIKE

IT'S LIKE WANTING TO DISAPPEAR.

YOU WON'T HURT YOURSELF, WILL YOU?

I WANT TO.

The police showed up to check on me. My father said I'm toxic and dangerous. Of course, he's right.

I'm poison to myself and others, but not either/or. I'll only die if someone will go with me.

CLAIRE

They patched things up and started talking again since the time he sent the cops to her house on some bullshit suicide threat. She got a job at a strip club called the Red Tiger to make ends meet. The night he didn't come home, I knew he was visiting her there. I couldn't stop thinking about her panties on the floor of our bathroom. Skimpy little things like something out of a Victoria's Secret commercial.

Though I suspected his infidelity, I said nothing when he came home. I kissed him, told him I loved him and to remember to call whenever he stays out.

I drove to the Red Tiger, went in, and ordered a drink. I sipped my vodka tonic and waited. The booze was cheap and the glass was dirty. I do understand the appeal of these establishments though. Every man has a creature inside him that craves a disaster and places like this are full of disasters waiting to happen. Drug addiction. Sexually transmitted diseases. Murder-suicide. Take your pick.

She took the stage. I almost didn't recognize her with all the makeup. In the dim lights, she even looked tan. Her body was tight, as I imagined it would be, and she moved with ghostly elegance.

Her eyes are closed. Her hair crashes over her neck and shoulders. When she opens her eyes, she sees me and smiles. The bitch smiles. And she waves. Like everything's oh-fucking-kay.

I smile back and when she's done getting naked, I call her over.

"Hey, what's up?" she says all saccharine sweet. She hugs me and I try not to cringe.

"I guess I had to see it to believe it. You doing a thing like this."

She shrugs.

"Anyway, do you need a ride home?"

"Okay, sure." She's so trusting, I almost feel bad for her.

I stay until the end of her shift and lead her out to my car.

"Do you like your new job?" I ask.

She smiles. "Honestly? I think I love it."

"Is it the attention?"

"When you put it that way it sounds so shallow, but yeah, I guess it's the attention."

I turn on some music and roll the windows down. A scent clings to her, like sweat and the kind of cheap perfume my mother used to wear. Reminds me of pine trees and mildew. I can't remember if Dominic ever came home with that stink, but that doesn't mean anything.

"I thought you were out of our lives," I say. "After he sent the police to your house."

She shrugs. "He was just worried about me."

"Of course he was."

I drive down Route 1, away from her place, toward our place.

"I think you're going the wrong way."

"I'm not."

"No, seriously, my house is in the opposite direction."

"You don't want to come hang out?"

"I'm honestly beat. Dancing takes a lot out of you."

"I bet."

"Are you…are you gonna turn around?"

I smile at her and make sure it comes across as cold as possible. I want her to know the disaster she's anticipated her entire life has finally come.

"I want to go home. Please."

I crank up the music, sing along to lyrics. She stares at me, her eyes wide and darting.

"What are you doing? What are you…"

I backhand her across the console and turn down the stereo.

"From here on out, you only speak when spoken to. This is my car, my rules."

A sob bubbles up from her throat.

I reach beneath my seat and pull out my handgun, a

nine-millimeter piece even Dominic doesn't know I own. I train the weapon on her.

"Even though I'm driving, I'm pretty sure I could hit you from here. Are you going to give me any more trouble?"

She croaks out something like a "no."

I keep the gun pointed toward her as I drive home. Her tears are better than music.

BRIAN

I don't know what kind of sick shit is going down at Dominic and Claire's, but my wife spending all her time over there after our separation is not fucking cool. And I've heard she's stripping. The idea of a bunch of other guys' eyes on her rubs me all sorts of wrong.

I don't even want to think about her giving lap dances. Greasy-fingered old men touching her ass, her tits pressed in their faces.

The night I hit her we were both hammered. I was too drunk to get it up and she started laughing. When I asked her to stop, she just laughed louder. Like she wanted to piss me off. Well, mission accomplished.

Anyway, that's over and done with. I didn't want to hurt her and I'm sure she didn't mean to hurt me. She's just confused sometimes, a little crazy. Being with her can be a real roller coaster, like the ones at Six Flags that go upside down and backward and corkscrew.

Yet I love every fucking thing about her.

Anyway, I'm gonna go talk to her. Maybe the four of us can figure shit out and get things back on track. I get out of my car, walk up to their front door and knock.

DOMINIC

I got my collision, a big, nasty four-car pile-up.

Claire came home holding Nora at gunpoint.

"Honey, what's going on?"

"Don't 'honey' me. Go to our room and take off your clothes."

"Where did you get the gun?"

"I don't think that matters, does it?"

I nodded and went to the bedroom, my whole body trembling. The two women in my life followed. I got undressed. Claire pushed Nora forward.

"You, too, hot pants."

Nora started to disrobe in front of me. Even under duress, she captivated me. The scars on her arms drew my gaze and I remembered the time we made love and she forced me to lick them. I wet my lips.

Claire narrowed her eyes at me. "This isn't the first time you've seen her get undressed, is it?"

"What?"

"You've visited her at work."

I shook my head.

"Don't fucking lie to me."

"I haven't. I swear it."

"How stupid do you think I am?" Claire said, "I've read your journals. I know how you feel about her."

My guts collapsed. "Baby, please. It's not what you think."

Nora was naked now, like me. Claire examined her, then turned to me.

"Fuck him," she said.

"What…"

"Guess you don't have brains to go with your body. Fuck him. I want to see how you do it."

Nora took a tentative step toward me, black tears streaming down her cheeks as her makeup ran. My heart thudded like a fist against my breastbone.

"I can't," she said.

"You can," Claire said. "I know you can."

Nora cradled my head to her breast, cried as she held me. I wept too. My dick hardened, noticing nothing but the naked woman's proximity. My deeper self, excited in spite of the fear clouding the surface. She dropped her knees on either side of my lap and slid my length inside of her. Her pussy dripped, also aroused by the terror. Our relationship could only come to this.

We found our rhythm, alternating moans of pleasure and

anxiety. All the while my wife held the gun on us.

"I knew you could do it," she said. "You're doing great, showing me exactly what I always suspected. Every man is a cheating piece of shit. And girls like you prey on them like a cheetah chasing a gazelle.

"My last husband tried to run off with a little skank like you. She got away from me, but he didn't. I chopped his legs off and made him stay."

I almost shrank inside Nora at the revelation. Nora closed her eyes and kept riding me. Either afraid to stop or turned on by all this.

"Eventually he got away too. But the two of you won't."

"What are you gonna do?" I asked.

"Shut up and finish. I want you to cum for her. For me."

I closed my eyes. I didn't know how I could cum. My fear had swallowed the thrill-seeking instinct.

Someone pounded the door. The three of us started. I exhaled, realized I had been holding my breath.

"Who do you think it is?" I asked.

"It doesn't matter who it is. If you call out to them, I'll fucking shoot you. Now get back to it."

A voice called Nora's name. Her husband. He knocked again. Claire retrained the weapon on us. We went back to our deed. I doubted I would ever cum now. I doubted I would ever cum again.

"Come on," Nora whispered. "Pretend she's not even here. Just think about me. We can do this."

"That's cute, but I'm right here."

She crossed the room, snaked an arm around Nora's midsection and cupped a breast. She pressed the pistol's muzzle to Nora's head. Moaned with us.

More pounding on the door. My cock grew harder. Both women's faces contorted in pleasure. A loud bang and I heard the door tear from its hinges.

"Fuck." I groaned and came inside her.

Claire spun to face the intruder.

"What the shit?" Brian said.

Claire fired. Brian's face disappeared behind a cloud of blood.

Nora screamed and dismounted. We all stared down the hallway. The top of her husband's head was gone, a cavernous red hole in its place, leaking clumps of hairy skull and brain tissue. His hands twitched with the remnants of life.

Claire went to him. She reached out with her free hand and caressed the ruined remains of his face.

"I'm sorry," she said. "You deserved better."

"The hell he did," Nora said. "You have no idea how he treated me."

Claire turned, raised the gun, and shot Nora in the face. She moved quickly as I sat naked and shivering on the bed. She planted the weapon in Brian's hand. Lifted Nora's body and threw the dress back on over her, putting her arms through the sleeves. As she did it, she hummed a cheerful tune.

"You might want to get dressed," she said.

I did as I was told. As I pulled my pants up, my penis hard again, and everything made sense.

My wife worked. An artist, a force of chaos, yes, but calculated. Though I did love her, I always thought she was too much of a good girl for me and sometimes wondered what drew me to her. I understood now. Boy, did I ever. She is perfect darkness. Meticulous, brutal, nothing like the dead woman on the floor.

I finished getting dressed and put my arms around her. She didn't resist. Our neighbor came down.

"Is everything okay?" he asked.

"Call the police," Claire said.

He nodded and ran up the stairs to do just that. Sirens already approaching.

"Why didn't you tell me?" I asked her.

"Tell you what?"

"That this is who you are, that you're so fucking…"

"What?"

"Amazing. Dangerous."

"Is that what you've wanted from me?"

"It's all I've ever wanted."

"Is that why…" She pointed at the dead woman.

"Yes, but…"

"How many times?"

"Twice. Once at the beginning of our relationship. The other time was tonight."

She giggled, cooed and rested her head against mine. Our embrace tightened.

Video Inferno

Maybe it was just the drugs, but this was all kind of thrilling.

Clark's hands upon me as I straddled him.

My husband filming me with his brand new HD video camera.

Kevin had asked me to fuck his friends before. Looked at me like I was beautiful whenever I did. Clark and I had been together before behind Kevin's back. And I loved him.

Would Kevin notice something about the way I made love to Clark? Would the camera pick up that different something, display it for the world? For Kevin. I let the excitement overtake the fear.

A raw animal spirit stirred within me at each inch of exposed skin. I focused on Clark who stared up at me in adoration from his spot on our leather couch. I could tell he was scared, too. Kevin uttered encouragement, but I barely heard him. I peeled off Clark's pants. I took him into my hands and wrapped my mouth around him. Kevin went silent, but I could feel the camera documenting my long-buried desires.

"Oh God..." Clark said, and I released him, delaying *his* release, and peered past the lens, into Kevin's eyes.

We hadn't fucked in almost a year. He only got off on the voyeurism.

I wondered what would happen if I told him how I felt about Clark. It was more than sex. It was spiritual. We were equals. I glanced over my shoulder at him, then returned my gaze to Kevin.

"Is this what you want to watch?" I asked and again the

thought of revealing this act had meaning. I didn't, because I still feared him.

He licked his lips, put a hand on his crotch and caressed himself through his pants. "Do it," he said. "I want you to fuck him."

I dropped a knee on either side of Clark's lap and guided him inside me, all the while aware of the cool black lens observing and documenting our transgression.

In my dream, my abdomen burned as if something with claws was trying to rip its way out. I shot up in my bed, throwing the comforter off of me.

The pain persisted.

White hot.

I wrapped my arms around my belly, which was swollen as if something wriggled inside of me. I screamed at the discovery, at the agony, at the fact I was alone.

How long was I out?

Where's Kevin?

Did he leave me because he saw my feelings for Clark in the video?

My stomach and groin flared, and I staggered out of bed.

I burst into the bathroom and flicked on the light. Bony features pressed against my swollen flesh, stretching my skin to grotesque lengths. I dropped my panties and crouched in the bathtub, seized with panic and turned on warm water.

New pain flamed between my thighs. I howled in agony as my gut shredded open. Dark blood filled the tub.

I opened my eyes. A red, cavernous tear occupied the space where my vulva had been and claw marks lined the insides of my legs. Chewed remnants of my labia floated.

A creature crawled in the gore and shallow water, like a large crawfish: spiny limbs, antennae, and a rock-hard shell. Wiry tails lashed the bloody water. Black orbs for eyes. An aberrant life form spawned by the nightmare of my life.

I woke up screaming, reaching down between the sheets to ensure my loins were intact.

They were, but I worried about my sanity.

Kevin stirred beside me. He said, "What the fuck is wrong with you?"

His beady little eyes glared. I decided I hated him more than anything.

"What?" he said.

I got out of bed and went in the bathroom to cry. He never checked on me.

Maybe it was the drugs. Maybe we got bad shit, but I don't think so.

The dream haunted me as I sat in my gray, secluded cubicle at the call center. Every time I closed my eyes, the crustacean's black eyes stared back at me.

I tried to focus on my work, through exhaustion and paranoia.

The dream didn't feel like my usual nightmares. I experienced pain. I couldn't help but think it was somehow related to my recorded encounter with Clark. Like fucking him in front of Kevin, under the scrutiny of that camera awakened me to the horror of my existence. This day-to-day bondage I agreed to enter.

An incoming call lit up my extension and broke me out of my thoughts.

"Thank you for calling K and V, this is Alicia, how may I help you?"

"Alicia," said a whispered voice on the line. "What a wonderful name."

Something about the voice's tone made me uncomfortable, but I tried to maintain a professional demeanor. "Thank you, sir, and may I have your name?"

Soft laughter. "I just called to tell you I enjoyed your performance the other night. On the video."

I tensed with alarm. "How'd you get this number?"

He laughed again. "I wish you were here with me now. The things I could do to you…"

"You're calling me at work. This call is being recorded."

"Come on, sweetie, I thought you were an exhibitionist."

I hung up. Tremors jolted through my body. The last thing

I needed was a stalker. I left my cubicle and went into Buck McKinsey's office. He stared at his computer screen with bleary eyes. He raised his gaze when I stopped in front of his desk.

He said, "Alicia."

I took a breath and folded my hands. "Buck, I need to go home early today. Can you swing it?"

"Ah, Alicia, I..."

"Please. It's important. Family-related."

"Fine, but you'll have to use your PTO."

I nodded, gave him a hasty goodbye, and headed for the exit.

In the parking lot, the surveillance cameras all seemed trained on me, shattering all illusions of privacy. I broke into a run.

"I want you to take the videos down."

Kevin's eyes widened. He sat on the couch, right in the spot where I fucked Clark. Where I fucked all of his friends.

"Why? I don't get it."

I wouldn't expect you to, I almost said. I told him about the phone call. I left out the part about the crawfish baby.

"Holy shit," he said, genuine worry in his eyes and I thought our relationship had some inkling of hope. His expression reminded me of the past, back when I believed he still loved me and saw me as more than a plaything. He put a gentle hand on my arm.

"You okay?"

I nodded. "Yeah, just a little shaken up."

He got to his feet and went to his study. "I'll take them down right now."

This empathy wasn't like him.

He sat down at his computer and I stood behind him. His room was like an adolescent boy's, covered in posters of women with bodies so perfect, so tight. I didn't think I wasn't attractive. Our videos got enough attention and positive comments, and plus, I liked my body. But something about this room always made me uncomfortable, like I didn't measure up.

Kevin opened his account on the hosting site. He got to the

video of Clark and me, and hovered the cursor over the file.

"Did you enjoy it?" Kevin said.

I tensed and stepped back. Played dumb. "What?"

He spun around in his chair. "Did you enjoy fucking him?"

I tried my best to keep a level tone and said, "I did it for you."

He got up and put his hands on my shoulders, leaned in close.

"That's not what I asked."

I pulled away. "What do you want me to say, Kevin? We were high. You asked me to do it. Actually, you *demanded* I do it. Don't act like it's the first time you filmed me having sex with someone."

His expression didn't change. "You love him."

I jerked out of his grip and left the room. I'd never walked out on him before for fear of repercussions, but I didn't need this today.

"Are you seriously going to do this? This was never an issue before."

He followed me into the living room and stood in front of the couch where it happened.

"I wish I hadn't made you do it," he said.

I came up behind him and put my arms around his waist.

"Don't," he said.

Kevin slept beside me. He tossed back and forth. Groaned in discomfort. I wondered what he dreamed, but didn't wake him. For one, he'd be pissed. I also didn't care much. He wouldn't do the same for me. I realized that was important.

I remembered what he said when I woke from my nightmare.

What the fuck is wrong with you?

The bastard.

I hoped the guilt and jealousy tore him to pieces.

I sat in Candi's Coffee Shop sipping a sweet, caffeinated concoction. Wished the establishment hadn't banned smoking a few years back. A cigarette would go great with my latte.

I looked up.

The cameraman wore a black suit with white gloves and a shiny red shirt. A large, handheld video camera obscured his face. The lens pointed right at me.

I averted my gaze. I was being silly. He was just filming the street. Not me.

But he inspired the same dread brought on by the dream and the phone call. Like I shared an intimacy with people whose intentions were dark. Violent.

He still filmed me. I turned to my coffee, but couldn't drink it.

It's nothing, I told myself.

Still, I rose from my seat to leave.

A shadow fell across the window. His camera lens pressed up against the glass, scrutinizing me and reflecting back the face of a rotting corpse. Blood trickled from empty eye sockets and oozing lesions covered its face and neck—my face and neck.

I threw my hands up and screamed, spilling coffee. The café customers ogled me.

"He was…" I pointed, but no one stood outside.

After the ordeal at the café, I changed my mind about going to work. Kevin left for the night shift and I poured a stiff vodka cran. I went and stared at myself in the tall mirror that hung from the door in our bedroom. I looked at my eyes, thankful they were still in their sockets.

Here I am, alone in the dark, drowning my madness with booze.

I tried to muster the determination to dump the drink in the toilet, when my phone rang. My mission unaccomplished, I set the cocktail down, and picked up my cell from the bureau.

"Hello?"

"Alicia?" Clark's soft voice shook as he spoke my name, like whatever held him together could give at any minute and send him sprawling into the emptiness of space or the cavernous mouth of hell.

"Yeah, it's me," I said. "What's up?"

"I don't know. I can't shake the other night. It's fucking weird."

I wondered what he meant by weird. Had he dreamed of

crawfish babies, too? Had he been called by people he didn't know? Was he plagued by an oppressive feeling that something dark and sinister was closing in upon him? Some sentient, insatiable void collapsing around his world? I exhaled and said his name, not sure what else to say. Do I tell him?

He said, "I just wish he hadn't pushed us."

Clark refused to do me on video before. Even told us he didn't one-hundred-percent approve of the videos we made, but that night, his date didn't show. He was high on ecstasy and down on himself. Kevin pushed us, true, but I wanted it. Told Clark it was okay.

Maybe it was the drugs.

Or the digital camera, bringing out our deepest selves even before Kevin hit 'Record.'

Crazy thoughts, I know, but I had a crazy couple of days.

"Because now I can't stop thinking about it... I can't stop thinking about you."

I considered inviting him over. Suggesting we run away together.

Crazy, crazy, crazy.

"Are you there?" he asked.

"I'm here."

"Well?"

"I don't know what to say, Clark. You know this is so wrong."

"I know. That's what's driving me so fucking nuts about it. We...had sex before...but..."

A sip from the vodka cran warmed my core, leveled me a little. We were friends and I had a responsibility to put him at ease. I hoped I could sort some of this out, too, by having a sounding board. I said, "Do you want to get a drink?"

"Sure," he said, the shakiness still present in his voice.

"When can you pick me up?"

"I'll leave now."

I hung up. My gaze drifted to the mirror. The man in the black and red suit stood behind my reflection, his face covered by the video camera. I screamed and spun around to confront him, but I was alone in the room.

I searched the house. Examined every room and decided I

hated every one of them. The whole house was a prison, and being here made me crazy. I'd let it become that way.

I ran out into the night and closed the door behind me.

"What were you doing outside?" Clark said.

I hugged my chest against a sudden chill. I said, "I couldn't take being inside anymore."

"I know what you mean," he said.

We sat down in the car, he pulled a cigarette from the glove box, and I asked for one.

"Here," he said, and placed a Winston in my hand.

He started driving and first we were silent, smoking away as the street lamps illuminated the ugly, prefabricated homes of our suburb. They seemed uglier tonight, like a cheap set in an old science fiction movie where people lived out dreams written for them by otherworldly forces and their true dreams lay buried beneath this false existence.

"What are you thinking about?" he said.

I blew my cigarette smoke toward the cracked window. I said, "You don't want to know."

"I do, though," he said in a way that made me fall in love with him even more.

I held to the torturous silence. Could I tell him I dreamed I gave birth to a monster. How sure I was the monster was more than a dream? That a ghost with a camera for a face was stalking me? That I loved him?

"I want to drive," I said.

"Are you sure?"

I flicked the cigarette out the window. It flew in the wind, sparking like a tiny firework, before crashing to a final resting place on the pavement. "It'll help me collect my thoughts."

He nodded. We pulled over.

Shaded in darkness, I couldn't see all his features, but the dread he inspired was unmistakable. He aimed his camera eye at me across the street.

I'd had enough. I approached him, hands balled into fists, my jaw firm. "Hey! What the hell is your problem?"

Clark called after me but I ignored him. I pulled the camera down to reveal the face of a boy in his late teens, not a whole lot younger than me. Dressed in casual clothing, the outfit was all wrong. He braced himself as if he expected me to hit him.

"I'm sorry," he said. "I was just out here filming. I just like to capture everything."

I wondered how I mistook him for the ghostly voyeur.

Because everyone's a voyeur.

Everyone's watching.

Clark came up behind me and asked, "Is everything all right?"

The kid trembled.

"I'm sorry, Miss."

"Forget it," I said, then to Clark, "Forget it. Let's just go."

We went back to the car and I slid into the driver's seat, loving the control, how it centered me.

We never did go for that drink. I drove us toward the outskirts of town. The rumbling engine sent pleasant waves through my body, reminding me of the ecstasy. We had the windows down and the radio blasted Orgy's *Candyass*, an album only he and I remembered. Clark sang along. A perfect moment I hoped would last forever.

I slowed to a halt and parked on a cliff that overlooked the river on Clark's side. On my side of the car were the road and a hill covered in trees.

"What was that all about?" he said.

"I just wanted to get out. That's all."

"Not that, the boy with the camera."

I hesitated. "Can I have another cigarette first?"

He handed me one and I told him everything. The words flowed like stream-of-consciousness poetry, like they were coming from somewhere else. A place only the cameras could see, perhaps.

"I'm surprised his only reaction was regret," Clark said. He knew about Kevin's temper, the fights that led to my outright fear of my husband. "Holy fuck, Alicia."

"I know."

"Do you think that dream means anything?" He lit a cigarette for himself.

"I've never been the type to think dreams mean much of anything." The sentence seemed to come from that same dark place, made me physically ill saying it. I listened to the faint, gentle sound of the water. A few miles down lay treacherous rapids. "It's like that monster, that crab baby, was the offspring of my life with Kevin. Like, we could only produce perversion together. I don't think I want to be his wife anymore."

"Don't say that, Alicia. You don't mean it."

I thought about the river again, the gentle flow, the violent rapids. Always moving. Never stagnant.

"I do."

We drove back at three-thirty in the morning.

We got closer to my house. I almost told Clark I intended to keep driving and to never stop. The idea of going back home, no matter the cause, horrified me in some primal way I couldn't even begin to fathom.

Kevin's truck was in the driveway. I cursed. I'd expected him to still be at his night security job.

"Is he going to be pissed you were out all night?" Clark asked.

"Yeah, but I'll deal."

He put his hand on my leg. "Do you want me to go in with you?"

"No."

Worry creased his features.

"I need to do this alone. I'll call you later. I'll be fine."

I kissed him.

Our lips separated.

He said, "I'll stay out here until I know you're safe."

Once I entered the house, familiar music played from Kevin's study, accompanied by the unmistakable sound of my passionate moans. Entering his office and seeing me naked on his computer screen, casting seductive glances back and forth from Clark to the camera confirmed he was watching the video from the other night.

Kevin's arm shuffled up and down. At the base of the chair,

his pants were around his ankles. I froze. I couldn't speak. Over his shoulder, on the monitor, I grasped Clark by the throat and grinded against him. I blinked myself out of my trance and said, "Kevin."

He didn't respond and I thought for some crazy reason he couldn't. The images hypnotized him, stripped away his autonomy, and turned him into a masturbating somnambulist.

I said his name a little louder, but he kept jerking off and continued to ignore me.

I walked across the room.

Blood and semen covered his raw cock. His hand moved faster than humanly possible. His eyes were gone, replaced with dark, bloody sockets. He whispered something over and over again, an indecipherable chant in some esoteric tongue, through a mouth lined with strands of viscous drool.

I backed away. Scream lodged in my throat.

I wished I had never returned home. Feared I wouldn't escape. Even if I did, the image of Kevin reduced to a puppet of lust and pain would haunt me forever.

I staggered into the living room, my legs like jelly, my pulse pounding in my ears. The scream tried in vain to expel. I spun around to run for the front door, and the cameraman blocked my path, lens transfixed upon me. I froze, caught in the focus of his all-seeing gaze, clenched in the grip of cosmic dread as if his camera was the eye of the world. His footage entertained the raving mob.

The cry wanted to explode from me. The audio from the other room grew deafening as Clark and I drew closer to our climax. He began to lower his device. I feared whatever I'd see would be horrible, something that would scar me to the marrow, but yet I couldn't turn away. From the video, the sound of my orgasm filled the house. I screamed with it. The camera lowered to reveal a gaping bloody hole. Deep red flowed, a waterfall of gore soaking his suit, splattering the carpet.

His camera dropped and I stopped screaming. I turned. Kevin stood before me, mangled genitals in hand.

I bypassed them both, headed for the master bedroom.

I entered and screamed again. Eyes now peeked through

bloody cracks in the walls and on the bed body doubles of Kevin and me pressed together and writhed in red-soaked sheets. We became less like ourselves and more a lumpy mass of flesh and hair. The eyes looked on, the image transmitting to some perverse collective mind.

The deliberate approach of the cameraman's footsteps echoed just in the hallway. I ran past the eyes, past the mutilated avatars of Kevin and me. Into the bathroom, locking the door behind me. My eyes found the small window above the sink, my only escape to the outside, where Clark waited.

A shriek tore my attention to the bathtub. The thing from my dream scuttled along the tub's edge, regarding me with black eyes and baring jagged mandibles. My nightmare offspring pounced and latched onto my face.

I tried in vain to pry the legs free.

A fecal smell made me gag.

I thrashed, knocking toothbrushes and toiletries to the tile below. Someone banged on the door.

I fought without hope. Only an animal instinct to survive drove me.

I locked my fingers underneath the creature's shell, spines digging into my hands, tearing skin. The grip on my face too firm. My mind raced trying to find an alternate solution. I refused to die.

I bit into the abdomen. Chewed a chunk out of the softer flesh. Bitter blood stung my mouth, but I gnawed until the creature howled and loosened its hold. With a final heave I flung the crustacean into the sink where it squirmed on its back, clawed at the air. I smashed the mirror and took the largest shard into my hand.

I drove the glass into its stomach again and again, spattering geysers of black blood.

I climbed out the window.

I ran to Clark's car.

Other doors opened along the street. Coming outside of their houses were more cameramen and camerawomen, the black lenses and plastic bodies of movie cameras shielding their faces. I screamed Clark's name as they closed upon me.

He pushed open the driver's side door and climbed into the passenger seat. I slid in beside him and started up the car.

"Who are they?" he said.

I ignored him and gunned the accelerator. More people came out of their homes on the outskirts of the neighborhood, holding cameras and recording our exodus.

But this isn't really an exodus. I'll never get away.

"Alicia!" Clark pointed to the sky above.

Red cracks split the darkness and the fissures were filled with eyes. I held Clark's hand, needing to feel his presence, to know I'm not alone in this new and terrible world.

Offerings

I woke to Kelsey gone from my bed on the tour bus in the desert on the night of the final show.

I got pretty anxious when I reached for her and came up with nothing but empty bedspread. I bolted up and glanced around.

"Kelsey," I said, my voice a whisper but loud enough for her to hear if nearby.

Maybe she's in the bathroom. A sinking feeling told me otherwise. I got up and walked the length of the bus. Shaun and Paul lay wrapped in sleeping bags on the floor. Everyone else was gone.

"Where the fuck is everybody?"

I stepped over my bandmates, and stuck my head out the bus's door. "Kelsey! Belial!"

I listened. The dunes were grayish blue under the night sky. No one yelled back. My bottom lip stung and I realized I was biting into it.

I let out a grim sigh and went back inside. Shaun propped himself up on one arm from his spot.

"What's going on, Chet? You good?"

"Everyone's gone."

Paul's head popped up behind Shaun. "Where'd they go?"

They both got to their feet. Shaun surveyed the inside of our almost empty bus. "You think they're out there fucking?"

A brief surge of jealousy took control, but faded under my anxiety.

"Something's wrong," I said. "We need to find them."

Paul stood, now dressed.

"I don't know, man," Shaun said. "Who cares if they're fucking?"

"I would, first of all, and secondly, I don't think they are. This whole thing is weird."

"Ya think?" Shaun hadn't budged, still wrapped in the sleeping bag. "We stopped in the fucking desert because our headliner wanted to go camping."

"Look, I'm going out there to search for them, for her. None of this feels right. You coming with us or not?"

A howl, then another one. From which direction, I didn't know. A coyote maybe. Probably. "Never mind, Shaun. Forget I asked. But I might just forget to close the fucking bus door on the way out. Let's go, Paul."

"No need to get all mean and shit," he said, pouting. "Give me a minute."

We stepped out into the desert.

The air was warm, like a campfire on a cool night, but it offered no comfort. Nothing ahead or behind the bus but an empty stretch of highway.

"We should split up," I said. "I'll take this side of the road. You guys search the other. They couldn't have gone far."

We separated. I tried moving quickly but the earth swallowed every step. A strong wind picked up, stirring up grit and the scents of desert plants I could never name. But there was something else: the smell of smoke. I climbed dune after dune, getting more and more uneasy, not so sure I wasn't actually in my own alcohol-fueled nightmare, but the sand spilling into my shoes and blowing into my face told me this was no dream.

From the curled, bright red locks that fell across her shoulders to the full, rich lips, the woman at Belial's side reminded me of his dead wife, Jessica Cook. Her form-fitting pink top and blue jeans revealed her body type also matched that of the late actress. Like most film buffs, I was more than familiar with Jessica's body. Almost all her movies had an obligatory nude scene. Four years since the Victorville Murders, I still did a double take. They could have been sisters, and from across the bar, I might have even said twins.

Belial led her by the hand to where I sat with the members of my band. It was the last leg of the tour and we were having drinks after a successful show at the US Airways Center in Phoenix.

"Meet my new friend," Belial said.

I raised my glass of bourbon, tried not to stare at her tits, and introduced myself.

"I know who you are, silly," she said.

Belial winked. "Shit, she acts like you're a rock star or something."

He introduced her to everyone else then sat down. He pulled out a chair for her and hailed the bartender. The guy behind the bar came almost immediately. His hair was a blue Mohawk, his black tee shirt too tight. I was sure he was a fan. Belial whispered something in his ear. The bartender nodded and shuffled to get the liquor.

Belial waved me over.

"What's up?" I scooted closer.

He nudged Dana. "Tell him about *your* friend."

She giggled. "Well, don't look now, because she's shy, but Belial and I left my friend Kelsey at our table. In any minute now the creepy locals are going to crowd around her and try to squirm into her panties. She's just waiting to be rescued by someone like you."

I fought off a grin, tried to play it cool. "Where's she at?"

Dana nodded toward a table next to a poorly lighted hallway. A sign for the restrooms hung above it. Sitting with her hands folded around a sweating pint of beer was another woman with red hair that fell in layers. She was petite, almost too young to be in a bar, and her slumped body language suggested she would rather be somewhere else. She stared into the contents of her glass, her mouth unexpressive. Despite this, I sensed something special about her, flawless, like the women who artists paint. Even from a distance, her skin seemed to glow.

"What are you waiting for?" Belial asked. "Rescue her before the locals chop her up into little pieces and stuff her in a trunk."

I pushed my way through a group of older guys gathered around the pool table and approached her. She regarded me with an almost bored expression. Her eyebrows rose, dared me to say something.

"Hey, I'm Chet," I said, and criticized myself for such a lame opening.

"I'm Kelsey," she said and laughed. "Is that all you got?"

"Do you mind if I sit?"

"Wow, you don't waste time."

I bit my lip. Belial and Dana watched the action unfold like eager lab students watching bubbling liquid rise in a beaker. Dana nodded and gave a thumbs-up. Kelsey smiled at her but stuck her tongue out as she did it. I'd left my drink at the bar and wished I hadn't. Kelsey was giving little away. She refolded her hands and stared up at me, getting some bizarre sense of enjoyment out of this.

"Would you rather I left you alone?"

She threw her arms out. "Come on, don't give up that easily."

I fumbled for something to say, but nothing came.

"You're not going to tell me you're a famous rock star or something like that?"

"Well, I…"

"Yeah, I know you are." She took a sip of her beer. "You're welcome to sit. Do you want a drink?"

I collapsed into the chair across from her. "Definitely, mine's at the bar."

"You thought I'd turn you down."

"Something like that." I found her even more beautiful up close. Her smooth skin and tiny mouth conveyed a fragile innocence, but her dark eyes and sharp wit gave away an edge.

"Sorry for giving you a hard time. Dana likes to take me to shows and set me up with the musicians at the after-parties. Usually they're douchebags."

"Huh. So what's the verdict so far?"

Kelsey shrugged. "You're too shy to be a douchebag. So far."

"Fair enough."

Kelsey waved into the crowd and a barmaid with bright pink hair came over to the table.

"Dee, can you get this guy whatever he wants?"

"Shouldn't I be buying your drinks?" I asked.

She winked at me. "Careful, Chet. That's douchebag territory."

I ordered bourbon.

"So tell me about yourself," she said. "And don't give me the Wikipedia version."

I proceeded to tell her how my parents were devout Baptists who told me more than once I was going to burn in hell for playing rock music. I told her about my only real relationship with a girl who left during the recording of my band's first demo.

"... and every song since has been an ode to her," Kelsey said with mockery in her voice.

"Not every song."

"Uh-huh." She propped herself up and kissed my lips. "Did you love her?"

I pulled back, tried to gauge what her reaction to my answer would be. Her expression seemed innocent enough so I nodded. "Yeah, I guess I did."

She smiled. "Sorry it didn't work out, though if it did, we wouldn't be having this conversation."

"So, how about you?"

"No time for boys when you take school seriously. Though Dana's sometimes tried setting me up."

"With douchebags, I hear."

Kelsey drained her glass. "So what's your plan?"

"For what?"

"For the rest of the night."

"I guess we're heading back to the hotel."

"I see."

"You're more than welcome to come."

Kelsey nodded across the bar. "Looks like Dana just made that decision for me."

I followed her gesture. Belial led Dana by the hand toward the exit.

I screamed Kelsey's name. Searched for a sign. Did my best to shield my eyes from sand. Hoped Shaun and Paul were having more luck.

I ascended a dune larger than the others and capped with large stones. By now I hurt real bad, my legs and feet dragging, my breathing heavy, my exhaustion overtaking my anxiety. Voices murmured over the next hill. The closer I got, the louder the voices. They were chanting a tune I recognized: eerie Latin verses that served as the introduction to Belial Crane's song, "Blessed Blasphemy."

A fire burned between jagged rocks fashioned into a circle. Four figures in dark robes stood around it, hands outstretched and palms turned upward. Hoods hid their faces, but I was sure the chanting came from them. Two naked women sat squirming beside the flames. An artist's cheap depiction of a satanic ritual, but living and breathing and real, happening in front of my eyes.

I was now aware of nothing else. I needed to stop this.

Kelsey's red, once immaculate hair was in tangles, her bare, pale skin covered in dirt and bruises. Dana sat beside her also ravaged. They were both gagged with their hands tied behind their backs, bound to a large spike in the sand. They whimpered under the cacophony of chants.

I picked up a rock. No time to go back and get Shaun and Paul. Whatever was supposed to happen would happen soon. The tongues rose in volume and pitch, became more layered; dissonant melodies within dissonant melodies. It also increased its rhythm. What happened next confirmed it: I was witnessing something sick and unnatural.

A red, mouth-shaped rift opened inside the fire to reveal a tear, in fucking space or time or whatever, a penetration into somewhere or something I had always taken for granted as impenetrable. The opening shone bright and full of fury. Spread. Became a great gash in reality's fabric. From beyond, wherever that was, something was coming. For Kelsey and Dana.

If I didn't move now, they were dead. Kelsey was the only person I'd connected with in years, a brightness in a world that hadn't been bright for some time.

This slaughter won't happen without a fight.

I ran down the hill, no clear plan in mind, except to use the element of surprise and the two-pound rock to my advantage. I slammed the stone into the back of one hooded figure's head. The connection sending painful vibrations up my arm. One down.

A second hoodie raised his head, revealing Belial's face all tight and annoyed.

He pointed at me. "You have no place here!"

"Really, Belial? How about this? Fuck you."

I kicked him in the groin; the singer went down. A dagger fell out of Belial's cloak and landed on the desert floor. As I dropped the rock and grabbed the knife, I made the mistake of looking toward the fire.

Fuck. What I saw was too crazy to be real. My parents raised me to believe demons, agents of Satan, existed and were at work in our world. Such bullshit, I used to think. Until now. A nightmare, straight out of my childhood, lumbered through that fiery window, a beast full of terrifying, blasphemous life. At the center of its face two black eyes stared down a large, dragon-like snout. From the back of its head, a mane of tentacles squirmed and curled over a torso sculpted and muscular and like a bodybuilder's, but scaly, brilliant with crimson. It had four arms. Four fucking arms, with hands hooked into claws. Its hooved feet dug into the sandy ground as it tromped forward.

Distracted, someone tackled me. The air in my chest left me as I fell. Death, Belial's bass player, lifted my head and shoulders and pulled me into a chokehold. Another hooded fuck unloaded punches into my abdomen. Through my clouded vision I saw the beast turn and set its sights on Kelsey and Dana.

I was fading. The dagger fell when I was tackled... *it's around here somewhere...*

I found it and plunged it into the side of the bastard punching me, pulled it out then rammed it up over my shoulder, and felt it penetrate bone and brain tissue. The prick with the wound in his side might still live, but Death wouldn't.

I ran to the girls, elbowing another of Belial's hoodies out of the way. I felt the beast's eyes on me, focused, intense, burning a hole in my flesh, reaching into my core, reaching for my soul, if I had one. I grimaced as I knelt beside Kelsey and sawed at the ropes around her hands, working quickly, hearing the footsteps heavily plodding up from behind. I cut through the last strand of rope, freeing Kelsey as the hoodie I elbowed nearly dropped me with a punch I never saw coming.

He overlooked the blade in my hand, until I stuck it in his throat. I grabbed Kelsey by the hand and brought her to her feet.

"Run," I said. "Move! I'll be right behind you."

She didn't need to be told twice, and was on her way up and over the dune while I yanked the knife from my second victim. Belial cried in protest. I turned and found myself face to face with my former hero. I raised the dagger, but Belial landed a hard punch to my mouth. I lost the weapon as I hit the ground. Belial sprung upon me in an instant, wrapping his cold, gaunt hands around my throat.

Life drained from me as the hands tightened, my arms pinned beneath Belial's knees. Dana's screams were piercing, deafening, and worthy of both, considering what was in store for her. I struggled to squirm free but no deal. I was going to die here, choked out amidst a bizarre ritual by someone who I once idolized. Dana would die, too, devoured by a monster from another world.

At least I freed Kelsey, I thought. At least…

Things went black, but only for a moment. When I came to, Belial was still on top of me but enraptured by the spectacle his grip loosened. I followed his gaze. Dana writhed in the beast's massive mouth. Its jaws clamped her midsection and tore out a chunk that included her rib cage. Her bones crunched, brittle as old plastic.

Dana's body hit the ground in halves. My stomach contents bubbled their way up. Last chance to wiggle free.

"Accept the sacrifice," he said while I fought him, choking down my vomit. "Accept the sacrifice…!"

A stone connected with the side of Belial's face and silenced his chanting. He rolled off me, onto the monster's feet. I shook my head to clear it, then turned to see who rescued me.

A wobbling Kelsey stood over me, still naked and looking like someone dragged her through the dirt. She held the stone in a tight grip, staring at the partly eaten remains of her friend, at the blood soaking into the sand. "Dana," she said, panting, "poor Dana…"

I got to my feet and took her hand. "Kelsey, we gotta go."

The beast glanced from Belial to Kelsey and me. Belial cowered at its feet, covering his face with his hands and screaming nonsense. It stepped over Belial and started after us. We turned and scrambled up the hill. I risked a look back. Belial's bandmates were incapacitated, two because I killed them. The thought repulsed me, even in my adrenaline-fueled state.

No words passed between us as we ran. The top of the dune loomed. If we could keep this pace, we could outrun it. Belial and his band could fucking die here for all I cared. What mattered was Kelsey and me, the two of us together, getting to safety.

We were so close, then I felt her hand slip from mine. She hit the sand with a muffled thud. I turned to pull her up but one of the beast's tentacles had wrapped itself around her ankle and was dragging her toward its gaping mouth. Distance didn't matter, not to a creature like this. Between its jaws, countless barbed tongues lined its cheeks.

I grabbed hold of Kelsey's wrist. It was like tug of war with a giant. I planted my feet but was dragged along with a shrieking Kelsey, to the monster's mouth. I groaned and gagged and grunted in protest. Kelsey wrapped her hands around mine, tried to hoist herself free, the two of us struggling against the hostile pull of an inevitable reality, and losing.

We needed a miracle and it never came. I continued to hold on as the cruel jaws devoured Kelsey a piece at a time. I held her hand even after the rest of her was gone. Sat there staring waiting for the same fate.

The beast stared at me, into me, scrutinized my heart's darkest places. I knew in that moment I was being examined by the infinite, that I could keep no secrets from it, that my place in the universe was like an insect wandering a long stretch of sidewalk.

I found myself screaming, a frantic shit-your-pants kind of scream invoking God, my mother, and every hero I ever had, Belial included, who had caught up and stood behind the creature, which turned to regard him, opened its mouth and roared.

"Give me what I ask," Belial said, seething and not backing

down. "I made the offerings. We had a deal. Pay up..."

What did this demon have that Belial wanted? He already had fame.

The monster started to wretch, its heaving forced. A large slimy mass pale in color, gelatinous, and shaped like an egg ejected from its jaws. Something moved within the object, something that wanted out. What I saw horrified me, but not Belial. He cried in ecstasy as the shell split and leaked green goo. From between the crack, a gnarled hand pulled itself to freedom. Belial rushed forward and grabbed the skinny wrist.

A human female emerged, shaky and disoriented. She leaned in closer to Belial. The fire illuminated her figure and the side of her face, and I recognized her.

Jessica. Jessica Cook, Belial's movie-star wife who was killed in the Victorville Murders, stood between her lover and the demon looking very much alive.

They embraced as the egg melted in the sand. The flames spread out from the circle, reached the beast and the reunited lovers and consumed them all. It happened so fast none of them reacted.

The severed hand bled through my fingers. Sinking loss pulled at me. I tossed the hand into the blaze with the rest of Kelsey, turned around, and ran back up the dune, away from the fire and all the things in it.

I don't think I ever stopped running. I don't think I can, and I don't think I should.

Hayride

Something with the feel of chilly fingers traced patterns upon Howard's exposed arms. The cold in the air this time of year was worse than the winter chill. A winter chill was expected. In the fall the cold crept up, striking only for only moments at a time before retreating beneath deceptively nonthreatening warmth.

Spotlights cast ghostly pale illumination upon the thick woods where Howard and the long zigzagging line of people waited to board the hayride. A DJ mix of gothic rock and horror movie samples played from hidden speakers stashed in the surrounding bushes. The scents of mud and dying leaves lingered in the atmosphere, broken occasionally when the long-haired Neanderthal in front of him shifted, sending a cloud of rancid B.O. wafting into Howard's nostrils.

Howard reached into the deep pockets of his jeans and fingered the grip of the revolver. Touching it centered him, made him forget the chill in the air and the poor hygiene of his soon-to-be hayride companion. Its cold certainty brought him patience. There'd be just one flash, maybe a moment of pain, and then it would all disappear. The chill. The smell. All the people. His loneliness.

The line moved forward like a singular unit, a machine made of flesh and Halloween costumes.

It had to be here.

It had to be now.

Mike called him the other day and Howard listened with something like hope as Mike said he was home on leave and that they should hang out sometime. Supposed to be tonight, but Mike bailed on him in order to spend the night with an old girlfriend. Howard wanted to kick himself, because he should've seen it coming, but instead it surprised him like a sudden gale of frigid autumn wind. Mike had always been a good friend and a reliable one too, unless the prospect of getting laid presented itself.

The distance between Howard and the hay truck closed. He thought he would be nervous. Instead, he felt more collected than in a long time. When Mike called to cancel, Howard hung up the phone, his body shaking violently, unceasingly. That was when he decided to die.

He spent all week leading up to the fateful call imagining what it'd be like to see his old friend again. He imagined them drinking in the parking lot of the Bone Yard, making jokes with the hayride performers and amongst each other, and finishing the night up at the All Star Diner. They would eat pancakes and drink coffee until sunrise.

These happy thoughts drifted away as if caught in a violent current as Mike said, "Sorry, but Heather called and, uh, you know, I haven't seen her in a while and I think she really misses me, if you know what I mean."

"Yeah," Howard had said. "I know what you mean."

He wanted to blame Mike for this, but as he climbed aboard the hay truck behind the smelly Neanderthal, he knew it was just an excuse to finally pull the trigger. Mike had been gone for two years now, so to expect that his once best friend would come home and solve all of his problems was a failure of logic. No, his life built toward this end over a long period of time.

The driver of the hay truck wore the checkered shirt and denim overalls of a farmer with blue-gray paint applied to his face to emulate undead flesh. He howled clichés like, "All aboard if you dare!" and "All the limbs that you wish to keep must remain inside the truck, otherwise they belong to them!" The driver burst into fits of laughter and warmth flared in Howard's core and his lips curled into an unexpected grin.

Howard had attended the Bone Yard Hayride and Haunted House since he was ten years old. His memories of his first time in attendance were still so clear. He remembered screaming and clutching his mother's skirt in his tiny fists as zombies clawed at the wood paneling on the side of the hay truck, trying to grasp at the passengers, and moaning in hungry pain. He remembered the howls of werewolves that seemed so close. He recalled masked maniacs frantically wielding chainsaws through the air. The rush pulsed through his body so intensely, he couldn't sleep that night. He lay awake giggling, scared and happy at the same time. He returned year after year, relishing the rush even as it lost its freshness and became one of nostalgia rather than one of discovery.

Five years ago, he lost his virginity in the woods outside the Bone Yard grounds to Tanya May Kramer. The sensual memory of her hands around his as the hayride commenced, of her lips on his as the truck came to a complete stop, of her warm naked body below his on that cold night made his heart ache in his chest and his penis stir in his pants. He lost her the next year to the affections of Warren Pryce, a track and field athlete the exact opposite of Howard in every way. When he finally got her to speak to him following the breakup, he managed to wrench a reason out of her. Howard was too jealous and possessive. A little of that was okay, she told him, but he didn't know when to show restraint. He agreed and promised to change. She told him it was too late.

Other girls came and went since her, but none he related to so deeply and none he allowed himself to fall for so hard. None of them stuck around long. But still, there was October and the hayride. While most people looked to the New Year for a chance of rebirth, he looked to the fall. As the leaves died and days grew shorter, he allowed himself to be born anew. But not tonight.

The hay truck topped the first hill and stopped. The engine sputtered and groaned as the truck idled and a hapless victim ran alongside, begging and screaming for help. For a moment, her eyes locked onto Howard's and he recognized her. She performed here last year. Something like recognition flashed in her expression too and she almost broke character. She resumed screaming as a man in a Sasquatch suit lurched out of the woods and pulled her kicking and screaming into the darkness. It was fake, cheesy, and absolutely perfect. Howard allowed himself to laugh. He stopped when he shifted his position and the hard steel of the revolver pressed against his thigh. The hay truck started to move again, farther down the wooded path.

It'd been a rough year. His mother succumbed to cancer back in April and he dropped out of college not long after the funeral. Most of his friends had moved on at this point, off to out-of-state colleges or into jobs that ate up all their hours, so he slept on the couch of Stanley, a coworker at the Black Horse Pub. Over the summer and into September, his loneliness like a black pus-filled lesion, he bought the revolver instead of registering for fall classes.

Howard rested his head against the wood paneling and stared up at the canopy of trees above him as the hay truck bumped its way down the dirt path. Black rubber bats with orange flashing lights stuffed in their mouths and glow-in-the-dark skeletons dangled from the twisted branches. A witch's bubbling brew gurgled over the P.A. system.

A boy no more than ten sat between his parents and was shoving handfuls of candy corn into his mouth. An expression of sheer, unbridled joy held the kid's features.

The boy's exuberance hypnotized Howard. He ignored the chill that arrived with a quick burst of wind that licked his forearms. The chill wasn't important; nothing was more important than what he was seeing. The boy reminded him of himself at that age: almost white-blond hair that fell in waves to his shoulders, beaming sky-blue eyes, cheeks that flared red whenever he smiled. The father took the candy away, but before the child could protest, the mother wrapped an arm around him. He nuzzled up against her breast.

Howard wondered if he'd go to Hell. He doubted it. He doubted there was a Hell because he couldn't imagine anything worse than what he'd lived through. He wondered if that were true. No, he thought, things could always get worse. They sure would for this kid with the candy corn. Soon, he'd grow up and lose people, just like Howard.

Howard wanted to take the kid by the shoulders, stare deep in those eyes, and tell him not to grow up, ever, because it wasn't worth it. It only led to pain and death and…and what?

The hay truck stopped and the performers wearing zombie makeup attacked, clawing at the sides of the truck and moaning for brains. Howard slid his hand in his pocket and touched the revolver again. He traced the curve of its grip, the cool steel of the hammer, the power of the loaded cylinder. One of the zombie's hands swiped at him and he ducked away, a yelp wrenching itself from his throat.

The little boy pointed at him and laughed. He just stared, his hand still touching the grip of the gun, his heart like the Hulk's fist against his breastbone.

The moment slowed. He heard nothing but his blood pounding in his ears and the little boy's exuberant laughter. Not laughing at him, he realized, laughing with him. They were sharing this moment on many levels. On one level, they shared it in the present. On another, they shared it in that the boy was experiencing it now as a ten-year-old and Howard did the same eleven years ago. Amid the staged mayhem, nothing mattered except this. Nothing mattered except this boy and his happiness.

The hay truck started up again and the zombies backed away. The ride went on. Men with chainsaws leapt from the woods. Giant plastic spiders dropped down as the truck passed through a tunnel full of cotton webs and purple black lights. A werewolf stood in the road, clawed hands clenching, jaws foaming, and brought the truck to a complete stop. The driver rose to his feet.

"Don't worry, all. I got me a silver bullet." He fired and the werewolf went running off.

The ride ended and Howard pushed past the Neanderthal, looking for the boy and his parents. He frantically shuffled through the crowd. They were nowhere to be found. He backtracked to the Neanderthal.

"Hey, did you see a little boy?"

The Neanderthal snorted. "Lots of them. So?"

Howard tried other people from the ride, but none said they saw the little boy he described. His heart still hammered in his chest, but it was good, and vital.

He walked down the hill, back toward the end of the line that zigzagged through the spotlighted woods. The face of the boy, full of life and youthful ecstasy, remained in his mind like some kind of clear mental photograph.

The revolver weighed down his pocket. It was there when he needed it, if he needed. He wouldn't need it tonight though.

He took his place in line, crossed his arms against the chill in the wind, and prepared to get back on the ride.

Worm Magic

See the dull suburban exterior of the Darling residence. Several cars pack the driveway and line the streets; all of them are of the upper-middle class variety. Balloons of many colors blow in the soft breeze, their ribbons clinging to the heavy-duty mailbox as if their lives depended on it.

A silver car pulls up onto the sidewalk, blocking the driveway. A bulky man in a cheap, ill-fitting suit gets out. A shimmery gift bag hangs from his shoulder like a purse, though given his size, no one would dare say so. He rounds the front of the house and walks to the side gate, where more balloons sway in the light breeze. The gate swings open before he can open it himself.

The pleasant-faced Nathaniel Darling greets the bulky man with a warm smile and an extended hand.

"Hey, Shane. Glad you made it."

"Wouldn't miss this for the world. Where should I put my gift?"

"Come on back. I'll show you."

With a hand clapped on the bulkier man's back, Nathaniel leads Shane into the back yard. Several people lounge on and crowd around aluminum outdoor furniture, some of them congregated on the patio, while others are spilled out onto the well-groomed lawn. Some hold beers, while others stuff their faces with stuffed mushrooms and taquitos. A large wooden plank stands at the center of the yard, staked into the ground like a half-erected crucifix. Over two dozen gift bags crowd its base. Nathaniel gestures to the pile of offerings and Shane sets his gift among them. He glances around, then settles his gaze on Nathaniel and frowns.

"Where's the special girl?" Shane asks.

"She's inside with her mother."

A third man comes over and joins them. He's hard-featured, fortyish, and, in black jeans and a tight tank top, underdressed for the occasion, though no one would dare say so. He's as tall and lean as Shane is bulky.

"What's up, Shane?"

"Brother."

They embrace. The third man turns to Nathaniel.

"What's taking Michelle so long?"

"You know girls."

He grins big. "Sure do." Then he gets serious. "You sure yours has been good?"

"Absolutely."

"Because everything depends on it. The company had a really bad quarter. Earnings are in the toilet. We've had to lay off half our marketing team and seventy-five percent of service."

Nathaniel spreads his hands as if the third man has pointed a gun at him. "You don't need to tell me."

"Just want to make sure you're sure. There's a lot riding on this."

Shane claps Nathaniel on the back. "I'm sure she's been good. Nate and Ruby wouldn't let us down."

The third man's face darkens. "Not Nate and Ruby I'm worried about."

"You're just mad your little girl didn't get picked."

"Uh huh. And she's paying for that."

Shane's features twist in a mocking expression. "How? By you making her High Priestess when you're ready to call it quits?"

"Come on. You know that shit ain't up to me."

Their attention turns to the plank towering over them and the growing pile of gift bags.

"Decent offering at least," Shane says.

Nathaniel nods his agreement. "Yeah, good turnout."

A dark-haired, sixteen-year-old girl sits in front of a mirror. A thick layer of foundation masks her face. Eyeshadow circles her green eyes, muddied lakes around twin wooded islands. Her lipstick glistens like freshly spilled blood. Her mother stands behind her, brushing the young girl's hair. Mom's absolutely beaming with tears in her eyes that could be of sadness, happiness, or a little of both.

"There's nothing to be afraid of, honey," the mother says. "It's a tremendous honor to be chosen."

"Are you trying to convince me or yourself?" The young girl's voice is barely above a whisper. Depending on the listener, its tone could be a cool sort of anger or trembling uncertainty.

"I just... it's still hard, even though I know it's for the best."

"I'm not afraid, Mommy. I'm excited."

The mother wipes her eyes and gives the girl's shoulder a squeeze. She takes a step back.

"That's my girl." She pauses, seems about to cry again, but she composes herself with a breath. "Okay. What do you think? Are you ready to do this?

The girl stares at herself in the mirror. She blinks as if fighting off tears herself, but her eyes are bone dry. A smile twitches up at the corner of her mouth.

"I'm ready, Mommy."

Outside, the people gather in a semi-circle in front of the stake. At the head of the group stands the underdressed man, his teenaged daughter, and Nathaniel Darling. The daughter of the underdressed man holds a bowl of water. A guitarist and flutist stand apart from the group, playing a happy song.

The mother comes out of the house, guiding her daughter by the hand toward the group. The people ooh and aah at the sight of Michelle Darling on this, her sacred and bittersweet sixteenth birthday.

The underdressed man dips his hands in the water in his daughter's bowl and shakes them dry. Michelle leaves her mother's side and approaches him. He smiles down at her. He grabs the sides of her face and looks to the sky. His eyes are rapturous.

"This is Michelle Angela Darling. Today on her Sweet Sixteen, we offer her pure flesh up to you, oh Lord Annelid."

"To you, oh Lord Annelid," the crowd cries in unison.

The underdressed man, the high priest, kisses Michelle's forehead and releases her with a gentle push into her father's arms. Nathaniel embraces her tightly. For a moment, everyone has doubts, fearing that he may never let go, or worse, that he'll turn and run, taking his daughter with him.

Instead he leads her to the plank, the stake, if you will. He begins to tie her hands behind the wood.

When he finishes, the high priest lights a torch and hands it to him. Tears fill the man's eyes as he gives his gorgeous daughter a once-over for the final time.

"I'm so proud of you, sweetie," he says, his voice choking as he fights back a sob.

He touches the torch to the nearest gift bag. The fire spreads, becoming an angry red circle at her feet. The flames rise, hissing and crackling as they burn the offerings. They encircle the young Michelle Darling, but instead of the expected cries of agony, the screams of protest, doubt and fear, the intended sacrifice laughs. It begins like the giggling of a young child, but the longer it goes on, the more maniacal it becomes, sounding like a stoned comic book villain.

The high priest shoots Nathaniel an angry look.

"You said you were sure."

"You fucking idiots. Do you think you're the only ones who know worm magic?"

Her laughs continue as the fire spreads across the back yard like infernal shockwaves from some kind of hell-sent earthquake. The fire doesn't die down until everyone is consumed. Everyone but Michelle, who re-emerges from the fire, glowing like the bioluminescent eyes of a deep sea fish. She leaves the back yard, not giving a damn about whether or not she steps on the charred bodies of former family, friends, and business partners of her parents. She exits the gate and walks down the driveway.

In the middle of the street, a redheaded girl wearing leather waits on a motorcycle. A black worm tattoo stretches from her left temple, around her eye, across her cheekbone, and stops beside her nostril. She stares at Michelle with eyes full of danger. Her smile is like a sneer.

"Is it done?" the redhead asks.

"Oh yeah, baby. It's done."

They kiss. Michelle hops on the back of the motorcycle. They drive away.

Above them, clouds shaped like worms writhe across the darkening sky.

Occupy Babylon

"What took you so long?" Eddie asked Michaela as she walked through the door.

"Nice to see you, too, honey. How was your day?"

"It was shit. You gonna answer me or what?"

She folded her arms. "I stayed late at the rally."

"What for?"

"More people needed to be fed than usual, so what? Do you have to interrogate me with these cameras on?"

"Do they bother you?"

"What do you think?"

"I don't think nothing. That's why I'm asking."

She shook her head.

"What?"

Michaela sniffed and sat down on the opposite end of their sectional. She fished the remote out from between the cushions and aimed it at their TV.

"What are you putting on?"

"The news was there today. I want to see what they show."

"Why? You already know what they're saying about you and all them protesters. Besides, don't you ever get tired of this shit? You know?"

Michaela held him in her sights. "People are dying of starvation. *In America.* This so-called 'shit' is important. Do you remember when we were kids? Crises like this only happened in other countries."

"You know, I don't get you."

She returned her attention to the TV. "I know you don't."

He inched closer to her. "I mean, I respect you and all. I just don't feel like we can do anything about any of this. Fucking shit happens, you know? It's just the way it is. Sure it sucks, but *we* ain't starving."

Michaela said nothing.

She fell for Eddie two years ago, mistaking his angry song lyrics for political statements. She later discovered they were hollow half-formed thoughts. Anger without education or eloquence. Hate spewed in every direction, rather than targeting a system that failed its people. Michaela realized this too late. They lived together. She wasn't welcome back at her parents' house because of her activism. Eddie didn't even know his parents and had no friends.

She had nowhere to go, and neither did he.

She flipped through the stations.

"Hey, are you listening to me?"

She sighed.

"Hey!"

"Yes, Eddie. I hear you."

"Well, why don't you say anything?"

Michaela stopped channel-surfing. A middle-aged, somewhat handsome man stood behind a podium in a street packed with people. The crowd cheered after everything he said.

"They failed us all, these men at the top. They failed us, and that's a terrible thing, but most importantly, they turned their backs on the Lord."

"Give me a break," Eddie said. "Who's this guy?"

"Pastor Brown," she said. "He's been coming to these protests over the last week and preaching to us. It's really inspiring."

Eddie looked from Michaela to the TV.

The pastor continued: "We have plague, famine, mass graves in our cities, and this has all been predicted. The End Times. You open the Bible, friends, and it's like reading a newspaper."

"Are you kidding?" Eddie said. "You hate religion."

"I do, but he supports us. He speaks for us and really believes in what we're doing out there."

The TV showed a close-up of Pastor Brown's face. "They must surrender the power to us. We can have our thousand years of peace if we win them over with The Word."

Eddie scoffed. "Sounds like a fucking nut to me."

Michaela shut off the TV. "You know what, Eddie? At least he's out there doing something. At least he's trying to make a difference."

"What the hell are you talking about?" Eddie stood and approached her. She started to turn away, but he took hold of her arm. "I'm doing something. I got something to say. What do you think all this is?" He gestured to the cameras placed throughout the room and the guitar leaned in one of the corners. "I'm doing something."

"Sure, Eddie, whatever."

Pastor Brown's hands gripped the sides of the podium as he cast his fiery stare into the crowd. Beads of sweat glistened on his forehead and red clouded his cheeks. His voice thundered, his presence far more intense than on television.

"You see, we're already starting to look in the right direction," he said. "We're looking away from the system, from its idols, from its false prophets. Now we have to look a little further. We need to look to the Lord."

Michaela crossed her arms over her chest and stared hard at the pastor. Though the television and word of mouth delivered much of his message, hearing it now confirmed she agreed with him on many things: the failure of the government, the corruption at the high levels spread far enough to bring the world to the brink of collapse, and the fact the people needed to fight back.

The only thing she didn't agree with him on was God. An atheist since high school, she saw the crumbling world as further proof of nothing up there looking out for people.

Despite this, she couldn't deny the pastor captivated her. He had a way with words and delivered each syllable with dramatic intensity.

"Is anyone here today feeling that emptiness?" he said. "Does anyone feel like they're being called to something greater? That all the work they're doing just isn't enough?"

Michaela's chest clenched. While she believed in her work

here at these protests, her personal life, the one she shared with apathetic, self-absorbed Eddie, *was* empty.

"Perhaps there are some of you," the pastor continued, "that if you died right now, you wouldn't be one hundred percent sure that you'd go to heaven."

She found the idea of heaven stupid, but his words switched on another part of her. Like an old television, though neglected and collecting dust, it still worked when plugged in.

She remembered her childhood fears of hell and the devil. Her Bible studies with her parents, lessons she rejected in her adolescence.

The dark imagery those passages often contained came flooding back to her in an epiphany of childlike fear. Grapes crushed during the End Times, grapes representing people. Oceans turned into blood. Fire fell from the heavens. Giant scorpions tortured those unlucky enough to be left behind. Everyone who ever lived judged according to every dark act they committed.

The people watched the pastor speak. Attentive to him because of a common enemy. They shared disdain for the people who controlled the world. Michaela thought about the quarantined areas, the plagues, the famines, and mass graves scattered across the world. There was no difference between America and the poor Third World countries she learned about in grade school.

"You're all doing great work," Pastor said. "But great work doesn't get you into heaven. So I'm going to ask, are you one... hun...dred...per...cent...sure?"

Tears tickled her cheeks. They surprised her because she hadn't cried in months, but also because of what triggered them.

"Let's bow our heads and pray. I know you don't all pray, but if you don't, could you please just be silent for me?"

The people around her bowed their heads and she followed suit. Just a year ago, these people—herself included—would have scoffed at the idea of religion, but things now seemed so hopeless. Things were getting darker, and Pastor Brown offered an alternative view.

"Now I'm going to ask, if any of you aren't sure that if you'd die you'd go to Heaven, raise your hand. Just raise your hand, and I'll pray for you."

Michaela raised her hand without thinking. Pastor Brown was immersed in prayer, and left time for others to raise their hands. He prayed for hearts to be open, for God to move and reveal Himself to these people. Minutes went by. Michaela's arm hurt and her head spun. The hardened adult woman and the scared little girl raged back and forth inside her.

"Now, if you raised your hand, I want you to look up at me. No one else look up, just those that raised their hands."

Michaela obeyed, and Pastor Brown peered into her.

In a mass grave somewhere, the first of the living dead opened its eyes.

Eddie groaned at the pamphlet on the kitchen table. On the cover, in bold letters, it said, "Am I going to Heaven? Free Test Inside."

"Michaela, what's this?"

The water from their shower pattered like falling rain in their bathroom. When Michaela didn't answer him, Eddie stomped to the door and knocked.

"Hey, Michaela?"

He put his ear to the door. He wrapped his hand around the knob and tried to jerk it open. It wouldn't budge.

"Fuck. Michaela!"

Michaela heard Eddie calling from the other side of the door, but said nothing. She sat with her knees hugged to her chest. The lukewarm water soaked through her hair and across her skin, offered none of the comfort she hoped for.

Her spiritual experience today went against everything she believed, everything she was and gridlocked her emotions.

Gloriously saved, according to Pastor Brown.

She strived to figure out what it meant, in relation to her previous self.

Did she now regret all her work, since she didn't do it in name of the Lord?

Pastor Brown had offered his ear for any questions. She feared any answer he gave would be skewed by his worldview. She wanted God's answer. Did God strip her of autonomy and call her forth to accept him?

This wasn't anything like the conversions she read about. Rather than a straight and narrow course ahead, she anticipated even more uncertainty than before.

Tears came again, and they didn't stop until the water went cold.

"Why didn't you answer me, huh?" Eddie kept the camera fixed on her as she came out of the shower.

A towel was wrapped around her wet body. Her hair hung dripping.

"What are you doing, Eddie? Put that camera down!"

"And what's this?" He held up the pamphlet.

"We aren't going to talk with that camera on me," she said. "We just aren't. I'm not going to be part of your goddamn reality show."

"Blasphemy, Honey." He waved the pamphlet. "You think God will put up with that shit?"

She put her hands on her hips. "Eddie, seriously?"

He laughed at her. Michaela stomped off into their bedroom. Eddie followed and kept the camera running. The towel lay on their bed and she rooted through the drawers of their dresser. He scanned her naked backside.

"Well, this reality show just got risqué," he said.

She spun around, covering her breasts and crotch. "Eddie, get out of here. I'm not kidding around with you."

Eddie threw the camera on top of the bed. It bounced once before settling on the comforter. "And I'm not kidding around with you. You're out all fucking night, and then you come home with this propaganda?"

"I had an experience today, Eddie. I..." She sighed. "You couldn't possibly understand."

"This Pastor Brown guy, did he get inside your head?"

"I'm not doing this with you. You're way too angry to talk rationally right now."

"Rational? The girl who had a religious experience is talking about being rational?"

"Maybe there's something to it, Eddie. If you pay attention to it, it starts to make a little more sense."

"You got to be kidding me." He threw the pamphlet aside.

"Maybe, they're right, and we're just cursed. We're doomed to fuck each other over, day in and day out, until the end of the world. And we're only truly good when we walk in Him."

Eddie leaned against the door jamb. "I don't believe this."

"I wouldn't expect you to, Eddie. You don't believe in anything."

"What are you talking about?"

"You act like you're so angry at the world, but you don't do anything to change it. You never support me. You don't do anything." She gestured at him. "You belong in this world."

"You know what? I'm getting the fuck out. That's what I'm doing." Eddie turned around and made his way to his office. He pulled some cash out of his desk, grabbed a video camera off a tripod, and packed up one of his guitars. As he reentered the hallway, he cast a glance back over his shoulder toward the bedroom. Michaela still stood there. "I don't support you? Fuck. I guess you forgot about me being there when your parents threw your ass out. I guess you forgot about what we have here."

"Eddie, wait."

He turned back toward the door and never stopped walking.

The hours went by and Eddie never came home. To occupy her mind, she picked up the camera and the pamphlet. She got into a groove and started cleaning everything. She unplugged and stowed Eddie's cameras. She scooped up articles of clothing off the floor. Ran the vacuum and took stock of her life.

Was leaving Eddie her only option?

Where would she go?

Michaela had a new faith now too.

When she finished, exhaustion took over her. She made her way back to the bedroom. She pulled Pastor Brown's business card out of her purse and decided to call him in the morning.

Michaela opened the door for Pastor Brown. An odor of expensive cologne hung around him.

"Michaela, how are you?"

"I'm well," she said. "I think. How are you?"

"Really good. Despite the way things are going out there, I'm grateful to be alive."

She led him inside. "Is it because of your faith? Is that why you can be at peace amongst all this?"

He nodded and kept his eyes fixed on her. He seemed to be studying her in hopes of figuring her out. Like he didn't understand how she couldn't understand.

"It especially helps that I'm able to share my faith with people like you," he said and sat down on her couch. "Do you live here alone?"

"No, or, well, I might now. I was living with someone, but last night we got into a pretty big fight."

"Oh."

"He was my boyfriend."

"You weren't married?"

"God, no."

"I see."

A long, awkward silence passed between them. She stared down at him as he sat on the couch. He held her gaze.

"Do you want some tea?" she asked.

"Do you have any coffee?"

"I do. I'll make that instead."

As it brewed, Michaela stood in the doorway to the kitchen.

"So, you're saved now," Pastor Brown said. "How're you feeling?"

"As you can imagine, I have tons of questions."

He smirked. "That's what I'm here for."

"Well, I guess my main question is what happens next?"

"Baptism is the first step of obedience. We can talk more about that later. You should also read your Bible every day. Do you own one?"

"I don't."

His mouth tightened for a brief second and then loosened. "I'll have to get you one."

Michaela brought him his coffee and sat down on the couch, careful to keep a space between them.

"What else is troubling you?"

"I guess I'm feeling kind of afraid and ashamed. Is that normal?"

"It is. When the Lord entered you, you became aware of your sinful nature and the punishment that you so narrowly escaped by being saved. It can be overwhelming."

"Why does God care so much about me?"

Pastor Brown's eyes locked on hers like a sniper's scope on an assassination target. "Because you're His child. You're beautiful."

She held the cup in front of her mouth like a shield. His stare made her uncomfortable.

"Why do you speak to the protesters? I mean, when I was a kid, I remember there being a huge divide between people like you and me."

"There still is, but I'm trying to close that gap. See, we've *all* been deceived by the Beast and his agents on this earth. His destruction affects all of us, and unless we come together, under Christ, we're all doomed."

"Makes sense."

"Did you hear that one of the encampments was attacked by a mob of cannibals yesterday?"

Michaela straightened. "No."

"They killed indiscriminately. Protesters, military, people just passing through were all attacked. It's happening in other places too. One of the fellows in my group said some of the mass graves were empty."

"What? That's impossible."

"Not if you believe in Scripture, honey." He inched closer to her. "See, the Bible is mostly a history book, except some parts are actually prophecy. They talk about things that are going to happen in the future. Well, it was the future to them. It's the present for us.

"It may seem bad out there now, but it's only going to get darker." He reached and brushed aside her hair. "Do you see what I mean? Faith is the only answer."

"What about working toward good? How do we have faith when things are so, excuse my language, shitty?"

"You ought to curb that tongue of yours." He took a slow, deep breath. "You showed wonderful faith yesterday when you came forward to receive the Gospel. You can grow that faith by hearing the Lord's Word. You must give in." He came closer. "You must let go of who you think you are." Closer. "And trust Him."

Pastor Brown forced her face toward his. His mouth covered hers, and his tongue snaked forward. Michaela flailed and tried to break free, but he wrapped his other arm around her. She jerked her head side to side.

"Come on, honey."

"Get the fuck off me!"

He yanked her head back. He threw her and got to his feet.

"You need to learn your place."

Michaela got on her hands and knees. She tried to stand, but he came down on her. He clamped one hand on the back of her neck. His other hand fumbled with his belt buckle. Michaela screamed, but no one would hear. Her drug addict neighbors were never home. She squirmed under the pastor's grasp to no avail. His pants dropped to the floor right before he drove a forearm into the back of her head. Her vision blurred and her face met the carpet.

Pastor Brown peeled her jeans off her in a matter of moments. The blow to her head had made her woozy. Time crawled. Her pants slid off. He tore at her shirt and rolled her over to view her nakedness. He giggled like a child and he pulled his cell phone from his discarded trousers. Aimed to take a picture.

Michaela wouldn't get any more opportunities to fight back unless she did something now. She kicked her leg forward and missed.

"Bitch," he said. "You made it come out all blurry."

He knelt on top of her and took her by the throat.

"You smile all pretty now."

Michaela reached up and took hold of his face. He started giggling again.

"The more you fight, the harder it's gonna be, Baby Doll.

You may as well just relax and…"

She dug her thumb into his eyeball. Made it pop and leak yellow fluid.

The pastor screamed and pushed off her, clutching at his face.

Michaela kicked forward again, and her heel struck his kneecap. He fell, still shrieking and howling like a wounded animal that learned how to swear. She got to her feet and stood over him. Her screams joined his in a chorus of pain and rage. She brought her foot down on the side of Pastor Brown's head over and over.

She didn't stop until there was nothing solid left to stomp on.

Eddie was halfway through the third song of his set when someone screamed. One of the new arrivals bit into an audience member's arm. More invaders shambled through the door and fell upon the crowd. The screams multiplied.

The scene changed from controlled chaos to the desperate pandemonium of people fighting for their lives.

Death came for them. It lived in the streets, on television, in their cities. But the others, like Eddie, carried on like Death didn't matter.

But it came.

With grappling hands, blood-filled mouths, and hungry eyes, Death arrived, and Hell came with it.

The people trampled over each other. Ran for any exit they could reach. Fell into the grasps of ravenous creatures.

One staggered toward the stage. Toward Eddie.

The figure resembled a man with skin an unhealthy hue of gray. A ragged, bloody wound leaked pus from its throat. Only one clouded eye remained in its socket. The other swung back and forth from its optic nerve like a macabre pendulum. The injuries should have been fatal, yet this man, this beast, walked toward him.

Eddie screamed and lifted his guitar over his head. When the creature got close enough, he smashed the instrument into the beast's skull. Blood, bone, and gray matter mixed with the splintered wood. Screams of fear and agony filled the room. A foul, metallic stench hung in the air. Eddie backed away from the horrid scene before him in the direction of the backstage exit.

When he bumped the door, he turned and ran. Hell followed.

Michaela sat against the wall with her knees hugged to her chest, skin cold and hot at the same time. She breathed in quick, hard rasps. The pastor's cell phone lay beside her feet. Pictures of naked women filled the phone. More than half of them she recognized from the protests.

Her thoughts seemed scattered to her. Every effort to move ended in her recoiling. Each time her eyes returned to the pastor's crushed head. The red spot on the carpet spread another few inches closer to her.

Footsteps paced outside her door.

What if it's the police?

They'll put me away forever. Use the murder of a pastor to demonize my movement.

She thought of what the pastor said about the cannibals.

Something jingled in the door lock. Michaela hugged her knees tighter.

The door swung open and Eddie tumbled inside.

"Michaela? Michaela, honey?"

He slammed the door behind him and stepped into the living room. He spotted the pastor's corpse and stopped in his tracks. Michaela let a sob escape from between her lips. Eddie glanced from the dead body to her. Genuine worry took over his eyes. More emotion than he showed almost the entire time they knew each other.

"Oh my God," he said. "Are you okay? What happened?"

He knelt beside her and took her into his arms. She responded, clutched him and cried hard into his shoulder. Tasted the sweat-soaked fabric of his tee shirt.

"Baby," he said. "What's going on?"

"The pastor came over," she said. "He tried to…"

Eddie nodded.

"That motherfucker was trying to hijack our movement. He

fed into our fears and grievances just so he could take advantage of us."

She pointed to the pastor's cell phone and Eddie picked it up. He flipped through the pictures and shook his head.

"Fuck."

"I know."

Someone screamed in the distance.

"Michaela, we need to get out of here."

"What do you mean?"

"I was playing at the Dive, and the whole place was attacked by a bunch of...fucking zombies."

"What?"

"I dunno, Baby. These people or whatever, they just started eating everybody."

"God, I heard that's happening everywhere." She put her face in her hands.

More screams, accompanied by agonized moans, much closer than before. Eddie stood and peeked through the blinds.

"Fuck me."

Michaela raised her head. "What?"

"They're all over the goddamned street. We need to go. Need to go now."

Michaela's gaze drifted back toward the pastor's corpse. The contents of the crushed skull made her stomach do a flip, but only a small one.

"Does it even matter?" she asked.

"What? Of course it matters. What are you talking about?"

"Everything's shit. All I ever worked on was hijacked. The world's dying. There's nothing left to fight for. Nothing."

Eddie got back down to her level. "Hey. What about us? Huh? What about us? Aren't we worth fighting for?"

Michaela wiped some snot from her upper lip. "Eddie, we fucking hated living together."

He ran his hand through his hair. "I guess we managed to fuck that up, too, huh?"

She stared at him, saying nothing.

"I love you, though, Michaela. I guess I was just too dumb to get it."

Hands pounded on the door and the windows, demanded to be let in.

"I love you, too. Maybe we'll get dying together right."

Now tears fell from Eddie's eyes. "We're going to die?"

She wrapped her arms around him. He rested his head on her shoulder.

And they waited.

The World Asunder

A series of loud thuds awoke me. I thought the noise was the porch swing, caught in a strong wind and banging against the wall of our safe house, until the screams.

Kyle met me in the hallway, rifle in hand. The day before, he told me how he missed playing *Call of Duty* more than anything else from the old world. I think he just liked shooting shit. He complained when we stopped seeing the living dead. He held the rifle close, eyes full of wild enthusiasm.

"Where's it coming from?" Kyle asked.

"Outside maybe?"

Kyle went to one of the windows. "I don't think so."

"Where then?"

He tilted his head as if to activate superhuman hearing. The beating continued. He and I glanced at each other.

"It's somewhere in the house," I said.

Caleb crossed his arms and drew his knees up on the couch in a near-fetal position. I placed a consoling hand on his shoulder.

Kyle searched the other rooms. He went to the kitchen and shuffled around some items, dragged a piece of furniture across the linoleum.

"No way," he said.

"*Help!*" A shrill female voice. I rushed to join him.

A door with a board nailed across stood behind a wooden table.

"*Help me, please!*"

Kyle's jaw clenched. He gestured with the rifle to the board across the door.

"No way," I said. "You take it off."

"Don't be a wimp."

"I can hear you up there. Please..."

Her voice shot ice through my veins. "We hear you. Hang on. You're going to be okay."

Despite my misgivings I pulled off the board and opened the door. A narrow wooden staircase led to a dank unfinished basement.

"Caleb," Kyle said. "Come here."

"What are you doing, Kyle?" I said, trying to sound firm.

Caleb shuffled into the kitchen.

"Go down there, see what's going on."

"Kyle, come on, man," I said. "Someone down there needs our help. That's all."

"Man, we don't know *what's* down there." He was being an asshole. Using his power and influence to push around others. His bullying had doubled since civilization collapsed, tripled since he got a gun in his hands.

"If something's down there, you're the one with the gun," I said. "You can deal with it."

He kept a hard expression on his face.

"Right?"

"Fine, we all go down there," he said. "You guys follow me."

The basement stunk of dirt and mold and each step kicked up a cloud of dust. A centipede scuttled out of our path and into a crack in the wall. What little light came through small rectangular windows.

The girl sat in a chair, her arms tied behind her back and one ankle fastened to one of the chair legs. Her other foot had come free and a wooden workbench with several tools stood beside her. I guessed her kicking the bench made the noises that brought us down here. Her blonde hair hung around her shoulders in dirty knots. Her eyes twitched back and forth, surveying her new company with a mix of curiosity and panic from her vulnerable position. I recognized her from Lower East High. She graduated the previous year, but I couldn't remember her name. Stacy. Samantha. Something else.

"Hey, it's Stephanie Beal," Kyle said and laughed. "I didn't know you lived here."

She stayed silent.

"Maybe she doesn't, man," I said. "Maybe some nut kidnapped her or something."

"No," she croaked. "I live here. This is my home."

Kyle snorted. "Then why are you tied to a chair like that?"

She turned her face away and I ached for her. I inched forward, eyeing up one of the sharp tools on the workbench.

"Hold still. We're gonna get you out of here."

Kyle stuck the side of the rifle against my chest. "Wait a second, man."

"Don't point that at me! What?"

Caleb wheezed through his nose behind me.

Kyle leaned in and whispered: "Wanna have some fun with her?"

I flinched.

"Dude, *no!*"

"Hey, come on. We can do whatever we want now and I can't think of anything better than *that.*"

"Just no, Kyle, no way." I walked away and resumed my mission of picking a sharp tool from the workbench to cut through her ropes. I settled on a hacksaw. "You guys gonna help?"

Caleb grabbed a handful of rope and held it away from her bound leg. I sawed through the restraint.

"You from Lower East, too?"

I nodded.

"How bad is everything out there?"

"You're the first live person we've seen in days," Kyle said.

She asked Caleb his name. He pressed his lips together and started working the ropes around her hands.

"She asked you your name," Kyle said.

"It's Caleb."

"Speak up."

Stephanie fixed Kyle with a hard stare. "I heard him."

Kyle grunted. A smirk spread across his face. I wanted to wipe it off right away, maybe use the saw.

We used to be friends before all this happened, but he was always kind of a bully. I guess I was, too. I didn't do much *actual* bullying myself, but I ran with his crowd and never made an effort to stop him.

Stephanie rubbed her wrists. She took my hand.

"I recognize you. You are... were... in my cousin's Anatomy class. Ray, right?"

I nodded. She looked at Kyle. "What's your name?"

He spat on the ground, rested the rifle on his shoulder. "Kyle."

We stood in silence. I wanted to say something, anything to move the conversation forward. Kyle volunteered.

"Why were you all tied up like that?"

She shook her head, locked eyes with me. Her irises were the color of leaves budding in the first month of spring, vibrant, shiny emerald. Her grip on my hand tightened.

"Let's get upstairs," I said. "This place gives me the creeps."

She cleaned up with a bottle of water and a washcloth and joined us in the living room wearing a pair of jeans and a yellow top. Caleb sat on the floor skimming through a religious magazine. Kyle knelt at the window, rifle in hand.

Stephanie glanced at the magazine Caleb read and tensed.

"Where'd you get that?"

Caleb looked up from the reading material, his expression soft. Caleb pointed to the end table. She snatched the book out of his hands and tossed it across the room.

"What...?" Caleb said.

Her icy stare silenced him. Kyle returned his attention to the window. Stephanie sat beside me. Her body heat stirred emotions I didn't want to feel.

Cleaned up, her skin shined, even in the poorly lit house. I thought about her hand on mine while in the basement and her glistening eyes.

She suggested we play cards.

"I don't know any games," Kyle said.

"We'll play something easy," she said. "Like Rummy."

Kyle rolled his eyes and sat across from me at the coffee table.

Stephanie explained the rules and we played a few rounds, passing the time without speaking much.

The door dragging on the floor forced my eyes open. Pale blue moonlight backlit Stephanie's outline.

"Ray," she said. "Can I come in?"

I tensed. "Sure."

I thought she'd sit in the rocking chair beside the window, but instead she plopped on the bed. I shifted to leave her some space but she nuzzled closer.

"What are you doing?"

"You seem nice and I don't want to be alone."

I knew how she felt. The threat of death loomed over me since the outbreak began, but death wasn't as scary as being alone, and this new world was, above all things, lonely. I wrapped my arms around her warm body. The swing rocked and coupled with Stephanie's breathing helped to me relax.

I woke to sunlight bathing the bedroom. Stephanie was standing at the window, staring at the long stretch of grass and thick woods, cut only by a single dirt road. The second-floor window had no boards. I came to her side, thought about putting my arm around her, but refrained.

"It's beautiful," I said.

She turned to face me, her eyes wet. "I hate this place."

I backed up until I reached the bed and sat back down.

"Daddy found out I lost my virginity over the summer," she said. "He went crazy. Started calling me a whore and threatened to kick me out. My mama wouldn't even look at me.

"He only got worse after things got weird out there. He started drinking again, staying out later and later. One morning he came home all covered in blood, saying the name of one of his friends over and over. *Alan*."

She gazed at a blank spot on the wall.

"He made Mama turn on the TV and we saw a report about those dead things in town, attacking people. He said one of them got his friend Alan and he just started yelling, getting madder and madder. Said whores like me were the reason God allowed this to happen. Said if he and Mama were gonna make it, they couldn't have me tagging along."

"He did that to you? Tied you up like that?"

She nodded.

"And your mom? She just let that happen?"

"I think she was afraid. Afraid of what was happening, but even more afraid of him. She never questioned him at all." She knelt before me, took my hands in hers. "I want to leave."

"But we're safe here."

"Are we? Your friend in there with the gun is just as ready to use it on one of us as he is to use it on one of those things out there."

"Kyle? Ah, he's a jerk, but he's not dangerous or anything."

"I don't know, Ray. Some people... you just get a certain feeling about them."

"Well, where will we go?"

"We can take my father's truck. He always kept its gas tank full, because he's a prepper."

I believed her. Kyle and I chose the house because the pantry had enough stocked canned foods to last a month.

"There's a back road that leads off this property. We'll go anywhere we want to go," she said.

"I don't know."

"You need guns? Daddy has lots of guns. We'll get them out of the basement, load up the truck, and... Well, think about it. I'm leaving no matter what. I can't stand to be in this house anymore. You decide if you're coming with me."

"What about Caleb? I can't leave him alone with   "

"He can come, too, if you want. Just not..."

"Just not Kyle. Right."

"You'll think about it?"

"Sure. I'll think about it."

"Great."

We ate canned beans for breakfast. Afterward, Stephanie got up from the table and went to the front door.

"What the hell are you doing?" Kyle said.

"I'm just gonna get some fresh air," she said. "That all right, chief?"

"As a matter of fact, it's not."

"There aren't any of those things out there," she said. "It'll be fine."

"If you walk out that door..."

"Cool it, Kyle. She's right. We haven't seen a zombie since we got here. Maybe it'd be good for all of us to get some fresh air."

"Well, I'm staying in here." Kyle plopped back down. "How about you?"

"I could use a stroll myself," I said.

"Caleb?"

Caleb kept still.

"Well, damn," Kyle said. "Who would've thought Caleb here would be the rational one? Fine, you two go out there, handle whatever business you gotta handle. If you're not back in half an hour, I'm not letting you back in."

I opened my mouth to argue further, but closed it almost right away. *No sense in escalating this.*

The sun hung over our heads in a cloudless sky. The outside air embraced us in warmth. I followed her around the side of the house to a rusty gray pickup truck in the gravel driveway. A chrome hood ornament shaped like an alligator glimmered in the sunlight.

I pointed. "Really?"

"Daddy was always a redneck."

"Yeah, no kidding."

"He and Mama took off in his Bronco. The spare key for this pickup should be attached here."

She crouched, reached under the driver's side door and came back holding a small sleeve.

I nodded.

"I'll have to leave at night." She came closer to me, wrapped her arms around my neck. "Will you come with me?"

"I... I don't know."

"I don't want to be alone."

"You can stay..."

"I really can't." She planted a kiss on my lips. "Will you come?"

"Yeah," I said, my mouth tingling as she pulled away. "We'll leave tonight."

"You'll have to talk to Caleb if you want him to come."

"Right."

She turned and put the key back in its place. We went inside, sure things would go according to plan.

Kyle stood and went upstairs with his rifle. Stephanie and I exchanged glances, and I tried to work up the courage to tell Caleb our plans. I opened my mouth and a gunshot rang out. A second followed.

"What the hell's he doing?" I said and went to the window. Another shot burst and a branch broke off one of the trees. "He's shooting at a tree. He's going to let the whole world know we're here."

I headed for the stairs. Stephanie caught my arm and squeezed.

"Let him do his thing," she said.

I nodded, but feared the gunfire would bring unwanted guests. I thought Kyle wanted the dead to come. Give him something to shoot.

I sat in front of Caleb.

"We're leaving," I said.

He stared at me.

"Tonight. We're going to load up some supplies in her daddy's truck and go. She doesn't want to stay here."

Caleb's gaze shifted to the stairs.

"He's not coming," I said.

His eyes widened.

"We're telling you because we want you to come."

He swallowed.

"Will you come with us?"

Another gunshot.

Caleb nodded and said "yes" under his breath.

"Hey. Don't say anything to Kyle, okay?"

"Okay."

Another shot, followed by a yelp of excitement from Kyle. The tree crashed.

We woke Caleb and he almost cried out in surprise, but I held a finger to his lips. The three of us went to the basement and she opened a large gun case on the wall. We carried as many guns and as much ammo as we could. After we loaded them in the back of the truck, we turned back toward the house to gather food and water.

Kyle waited for us at the front door. His exposed arms and chest bulged as he clutched the rifle.

"Just where do you think you're going?"

I stared into the dark eyes of my former friend and he stared back, down the barrel of the rifle.

"Kyle..." Stephanie said.

He aimed at her. "You shut up!"

I put up my hands. "Listen, Kyle, there's no sense in..."

He rammed the butt of the gun into my jaw and I pitched backward, landing hard with silver specks exploding before my eyes. Coppery blood filled my mouth and I gagged.

I lay dazed. Somewhere far away Stephanie screamed.

I tried to get to my feet, but dizziness forced me back. I feared the extent of my injuries, but I feared Kyle's next move even more.

"Sit down and shut up," he said to Stephanie. "And you..."

Something tightened around my wrist and pulled me up. Another impact shattered the bridge of my nose, and I crashed into the bushes at the foot of the porch. I coughed blood out of my throat, and spat into the dirt.

Kyle retrained the gun on Stephanie.

Caleb stood frozen in front of the house. I felt for the kid and hated him. I wanted him to help us, but he had every right to be scared.

"Now," Kyle said, "about that fun I was talking about earlier."

My heart fell like an anvil.

He prodded Stephanie with the rifle. "Get naked."

"No," she said, her voice a weak croak.

"Excuse me? I said, 'get naked,' and I can either let you live or send you to whore heaven. I think you better listen."

"Kill me. I don't care."

"No, no, see, you're not going to get off that easily." He took a knife from his belt. He snatched her by the wrist and held out her hand.

I screamed. He drove the blade into the palm of her hand and she howled.

My insides revolted and I gagged on more blood.

He pulled the knife out and got back on the porch. She clutched her bleeding hand. He picked up the rifle and trained it on her.

"Now, do as I say, or next time it's gonna be a lot worse." I approached, but he aimed the gun at me again. "Not so fast, Ray. You're ruining all the fun. Get back."

He shifted his gaze to Stephanie. "Now get naked before I get real mean."

"Go to hell," she said.

"Do it, or lover boy gets his brains blown out."

She pulled off her top and undid her bra. Her pale flesh glowed blue in the moonlight. She stepped out of her pants.

"That's better," Kyle said. He walked down, squeezed a breast.

"Get your hands off me." She tried to bite him, but he backed up.

"Hey, play nice now." He bit his lip. "So, how are we gonna do this? I can't put my gun down. Oh, I know."

He grinned. I thought again about removing his smile with a hacksaw. Too late now.

He pointed the gun at Caleb.

"You, queer boy, how about I let you have the first go."

Caleb shook his head.

"That wasn't a request. Now do it."

Caleb removed his clothes, tears in his eyes. The porch swing swung and landed against the house with a dull, maddening thud. Caleb thrust into Stephanie and wept.

Caleb curled into a fetal position on the grass. Kept mumbling something I couldn't decipher.

"You did great, boy," Kyle said. "Now get up."

He laughed as he came toward Caleb. Kyle helped Caleb up and shoved the rifle into the crying boy's naked arms.

"Hey, you liked it, there's no shame in liking it. Show's you're not a queer after all."

Stephanie kept her head high and chewed her lip. Blood leaked from the hole in her hand.

Caleb tried to back away, but Kyle put him in a headlock.

"Don't go running off now. I did you a favor; now I need you to do one for me. Can you do that?"

Caleb wailed.

"Hey, hey, shhhh." Kyle pulled the knife from his belt and held the tip under Caleb's chin. "Head up, son. I did something nice for you. Where I'm from, when someone does something nice for you, you do something for them in return. Now, are you gonna do me a favor or not?"

Caleb licked his lips and uttered something.

"Great. I want you to point that gun at Ray over there, make sure he doesn't try anything funny while I'm having my turn at her. Think you can do that?"

Caleb blubbered.

"Hey, I need to know now, boy. Are you gonna do me that solid or am I gonna have to ram this knife into your brain?"

"I'll do it," Caleb said, sobs tearing from his throat. "I'll do it."

Kyle nodded. "See, we'll make a man out of you just yet. Now, aim the gun at Ray."

Caleb complied. Kyle gave him a small round of applause. He unbuttoned his jeans.

"Caleb…" I said.

Kyle shot a finger in my direction. "Shut up. If you're good, maybe I'll let you have a go at her, too. That is, if you haven't already."

I stared at Caleb, tried to meet the scared boy's eyes. Willed him to turn and shoot Kyle.

Kyle's pants fell with a jingle of his belt. The knife gleamed in its sheath.

Stephanie cried in protest. She slapped at her oncoming rapist.

Kyle threw her to her belly. Knelt behind her.

"This how you want it, huh?" He clutched her hair with one hand and held his genitals in the other.

Caleb still had the gun centered on me. Poor kid was traumatized, probably didn't even know what he was doing.

Kyle yelped. He flailed his arms and staggered back from Stephanie. The knife jutted out his neck, half an inch above his collar bone. Stephanie rolled away from him.

"Caleb, shoot him," she said.

Caleb shook, woke from a trance. He pivoted. Kyle pulled out the knife, releasing a scarlet spray. He raised the blade and stalked toward Stephanie, gurgling obscenities.

"Now, Caleb! Do it now!" I said.

A loud report tore through the air. Red bloomed across Kyle's breastbone and the exit wound spat gore and bone on the porch. Kyle's eyes went wide. He put a hand to his chest, ogled the blood gushing through his fingers and up at Caleb. He gagged once, spewing crimson drool down his chin and fell against the steps.

My pulse pounded in my head. Didn't know if I was breathing or not.

Stephanie spat on Kyle's corpse. I wrapped my arms around her trembling body.

The swing swayed. I expected the walking dead to approach, drawn to the commotion, but I heard only wind. I smelled no decay, only the fresh blood of Stephanie's and Kyle's wounds.

Caleb still held the gun in a tense grip.

"Caleb?"

His eyes reminded me of interviews on television with soldiers afflicted with PTSD. He dropped to his knees and put the rifle under his chin. I let go of Stephanie and rushed toward him.

"No!"

The blast exploded Caleb's head in a cloud of gore. His remains slumped. Hunks of brain and skull rained around him.

I pounded my fists against the sides of my head and shrieked. Stephanie came over and put her arms around me. We held each other until the first bursts of orange lit the morning sky.

She studied Kyle's corpse. "Do you think he'll come back as one of them? It happens in the movies, doesn't it?"

"This isn't a movie."

I let go of her and walked over to where Kyle lay. Blood soaked the ground below him. I gave him a kick and his body stayed limp.

"He's dead," I said. "He's not coming back. I don't think anyone is anymore."

She examined her nakedness.

"I want to get dressed."

We changed our clothes and tended to our wounds. Afterward, I proposed giving Caleb a proper burial. I didn't even mention what we should do with Kyle. She suggested we put them inside and burn the house to the ground. I didn't argue with her.

We dragged the corpses into the house and started a fire in the living room. We watched from a safe distance as the flames grew and danced. The dead never came for us. I still felt too wounded to entertain the slightest shred of hope.

We left the house behind, still burning strong at midmorning. The porch swing fell off its chains and smoldered in the blaze.

We drove for a good hour into the countryside, the living dead nowhere to be found. Their absence brought no comfort. The events of the night haunted me. I wanted to believe I couldn't blame myself. I tried to think about other things: my family and trips to Sea Isle, snuggling with Stephanie in her room, but none of those memories stayed. The recollections of total powerlessness returned with a vengeance and guilt consumed me.

The sun shined, uninhibited by clouds. Its light illuminated the rolling hillsides and lush fields around us; its heat warmed the truck's interior. But with the world torn asunder, light and warmth only made me think of the fire and sins that would never burn away.

A Killing Back Home

The presence of Randall Sykes in the movie theater made Kimber De Costa lose her train of thought. She forgot the question, stumbled over a few words, and bit her lip. They weren't far from her hometown, but they were far enough for Randall's presence to be strange. Her gaze shifted to the questioner, a petite redhead with thick-rimmed glasses, in hopes of jarring her memory. No luck.

Brunshea leaned into her and whispered, "You okay?"

"Yeah, just..."

"She asked how you choose each cold case for your documentaries," he said.

Kimber cleared her throat.

"Sorry about that," she said into the microphone. "It's been a long trip. Each case I choose speaks to me in its own way. Either I identify with the victim, or sometimes, the killer, like in the film you just saw."

They finished the Q & A, and Kimber waited on stage. Randall would come to her. He had something to say, otherwise he wouldn't have come all this way.

"You okay?" Brunshea asked.

"I'm fine. We've got a visitor though." She nodded in Randall's direction.

"Someone you know?"

"I grew up with him."

"Damn, girl, you grew up like seventy miles from here."

"I guess I'm popular," she said and winked, as Randall began to make his way through the crowd.

He approached the stage. Kimber stood and folded her

hands. He said her name.

"Randall, what brings you out all this way?"

"Been trying to get ahold of you. Figured it'd be easiest to show up here. Have a second?"

"I suspect you didn't come this far to talk for a second. What's up?"

Randall cast a glare at Brunshea's imposing physique. "Who's this, your bodyguard?"

"Hardly. This is Brunshea. He's my DP. Brunshea, this is Randall."

They shook hands. Randall stared at Kimber. A sideways smile crept up the corner of his mouth.

"It's good to see you," he said. "How've you been?"

"Good. Tired. I'd like to get back to the hotel, actually. Can what you have to tell me wait?"

"Same old Kimber. Always down to business." He sucked in a breath. "Well, okay. Kid's been murdered in town, and well, your daddy, he's our prime suspect."

Kimber's face got hot. Something in her chest got heavy. She wanted to sit back down, but kept her feet planted.

"What makes you think Alejandro had something to do with it?"

"Christ, Kimber, he's your daddy. Least you could call him, oh, never mind. It's not my business."

"I'm guessing you found the stiff on Alejandro's property."

Randall's eyes widened. "How...?"

"It's not difficult to deduce, really. You came all the way out here to say my father is the prime suspect in a murder case. Alejandro owns quite a stretch of land, which would make his property an ideal place to dump a body. Either there or the creek."

"It was near the creek. Tied to a tree."

"Well, there you go. Tied to a tree, you say?"

"Yeah."

"Interesting. Well, as I was saying, the fact that the body was found on Alejandro's land would make him a prime suspect, especially since, I'm going to go out on a limb here and say, that's the only piece of evidence you've got."

Randall gulped.

"Right, so, the only part I can't figure out is why you're telling me this in person. You either just thought I should know, which a simple Facebook message would have been sufficient for, or you want my help. If you want my help, I'm not sure why."

"Well, he's got an alibi. Was with a bunch of fellow retirees around the boy's time of death."

"That still doesn't tell me why you need my help."

"Damn, girl," Brunshea said.

"What?"

"You're being…"

"A bitch, I know. Randall knows why. I got out of that town for a reason. I'm in no rush to get back."

"Damn it, Kimber," Randall said. "I need your help."

"You forgot something, Randall."

"What's that?"

"I only do cold cases. I can't interfere with your investigation, no matter how meager."

"We'd bring you on as a consultant."

"The answer is 'no.'"

Randall produced a weathered business card with his name, contact information and title, "Sergeant," on it. She stared at it, but didn't take it.

"Hope you'll reconsider."

"It was good to see you, Randall."

"Jesus," Brunshea said and snatched the card. "At least take the man's card."

"Right. Humor me a little."

"I'd rather not string you along, even if it's all the same to you. Take care of yourself, okay?"

"Yeah, you too."

They listened to Kanye's *Yeezus* on their way back to the motel. Kimber turned it up loud when "Black Skinhead" came on. She moved her head and shoulders to the furious beat as she drove. Brunshea turned down the music.

"You good? You look like you're about to hit something."

"I'm fine, Brunshea."

"Yeah, whatever. You don't look fine."

"Aw, thanks. You know how to make a girl feel special."

"You know what I mean."

"No. Yes. Maybe. I don't know."

"Never heard you so unsure of yourself. I'm gonna assume you're still tripping."

"Smart boy." She fidgeted, wanted to crank up the music again. "How much farther until we reach the motel?"

He checked the navigation on the phone in his lap.

"Nine minutes. Anyway, maybe you're tripping for a reason."

"Oh, and what reason is that?"

"I'm saying maybe we should help Randall out."

"Dad's the one that stopped talking to me, Brunshea."

"Yeah, but you *did* skip out on your mom's funeral."

"We were filming in Europe."

"Mmm-hmm, and have you even gone to the grave to pay your respects?"

"I've..."

"Been busy, yeah."

Kimber turned the music back up.

Kimber lay awake while Brunshea showered. The darkness brought her no comfort. She thought about her last conversation with her father. He said her success didn't mean anything if she didn't have people in her life she cared about. She told him she cared about him and her mom, and was very sad her mother had died, but she couldn't get away. The shooting schedule for the unsolved Oslo Slasher documentary had been brutal and marred by the elements. She told him she wished she could be there, but she couldn't.

"Well, if this is how you treat family, maybe you don't know how to be part of a family," he said. "Maybe you don't need to be part of my family."

They hung up after that and hadn't spoken since.

Brunshea walked out of the bathroom. She turned away from his gorgeous and glistening dark body.

"Guess I'm sleeping in the other bed tonight," he said.

"You're quite the detective. Maybe you should take my place."

He threw the damp towel at her. She laughed, despite herself. Brunshea got in the other bed and wrapped himself in a sheet. They weren't an item, but they sometimes slept together. Mostly they were just colleagues who didn't have time for outside relationships, and relied on each other when the loneliness got to be too much.

"Hey, Kimber?"

"Yes."

"Think about what I said, okay?"

She said nothing. Brunshea let the subject drop. Ten minutes later, he started to snore. Kimber couldn't sleep. She sat up and chewed her lip, then grabbed her cell phone and the business card off of the night table, and stepped outside. She turned the business card over in her hand, stared at the blank back of it. She stuffed it in her pocket and took it back out again.

For all her award-winning detective work, she couldn't figure out why she dialed Randall's number. Maybe it was the nights spent awake, whether alone or with Brunshea, where she wondered about the past, the life she left behind to do the thing that had brought her so much success. Maybe she hadn't completely hardened her heart to her father for cutting her out. Maybe Brunshea was right and this was a good opportunity to repair rifts, with her father and *others*. There were a lot of rifts to repair back home.

Whatever her reasons, she dialed the number on the business card. Randall answered, his voice choked with sleep.

"It's Kimber," she said. "I'm in."

"We're rolling," Brunshea said from the back of Randall's car.

Kimber pivoted in the passenger seat to face Randall. She used to hold a clipboard to keep her thoughts straight, but years of working in her field had given her an impeccable grasp on the right things to ask, not just to learn what she needed to know, but to create a compelling narrative for her films.

"Tell me about the victim," she said.

"Percy Wilkes, eleven years old. Mother left when he was four. He was raised by his father. Diagnosed with autism spectrum disorder and prone to wandering. Nice enough kid, kind of a pain in the ass though."

"How so?"

"Just… I don't know, he got in everyone's way. Guess people around here aren't educated enough to know how to deal with a kid in his condition."

"Did he have any enemies?"

"Nothing like that. Not that I know of. Just got under people's skin. Rubbed them wrong."

"What's his father like?"

"Holden? Nice enough guy, I suppose. Can't always hold it together though."

"He's lost his son before."

"Couple times. Was doing good for a while, after he made his house harder for Percy to get out of." Randall sighed. "Guess there's no way to stop a kid from wandering out in public, short of holding his hand everywhere you go."

"Did Holden ever get really angry at Percy? Did he ever hit him or anything like that?"

"No, nothing like that. Holden's the kind of guy who will punish himself before he punishes anyone else."

"How does he punish himself?"

"Sometimes he don't leave the house for days at a time. That sort of thing."

"And the mother?"

"No one's seen her since she left."

"Why did she leave?"

"Didn't have the patience to deal with a special needs child. Kind of a party girl. Wanted to keep her social life alive, I guess. Like I said, no one's seen her since she left."

Kimber paused. She glanced from the camera to Randall.

"How did Percy die?"

"Whoever… uh, did it… cut off his tongue, before they tied him to a tree. He bled to death."

Kimber turned to the camera. She kept her expression somber, but detached. It was a look she practiced in the mirror throughout college, when she wanted to be a TV reporter, before her love of investigative filmmaking consumed all other passions. The look served her well in these documentaries too. It lent a journalistic quality to what she did.

"Percy Wilkes's body was found on the property of Alejandro De Costa." She paused, partly to keep her composure, but mostly for dramatic effect. "My father. He's the prime person of interest in the Percy Wilkes murder case. We're headed to his home to find out what he knows."

Brunshea switched off the camera.

"Crushed it, girl," he said. "How much longer 'til we get there?"

"Just a bit farther," Randall said. "Few blocks."

"You call him?" Brunshea asked.

"No. It's probably best he doesn't know I'm coming." She thought for a moment. "As a matter of fact, it's probably a good idea to leave the camera off when we get there, at least at first."

Alejandro De Costa's five-bedroom house sat on a ten-acre swath of land. He made his money as an obstetrician in Philadelphia. Now a retired empty nester and widower, he stayed on his massive property because he had grown accustomed to the solitude.

Randall drove the cruiser up the tree-lined driveway and stopped in front of the home's arched entrance. Kimber got out of the car. Brunshea sidled up next to her.

"Ready for this?" he said.

"I'll be fine."

"I better take the lead," Randall said. "We are here on police business."

"Go right ahead."

They walked up to the front door. Randall knocked. A woman with bleach-blonde hair and wearing a cleaning apron answered the door. She gave them a weary smile. After Kimber and her three older brothers moved out, her father hired a maid. Kimber didn't remember the maid's name, but the maid remembered her. The maid's smile broadened.

"Kimber, what are you doing here?"

"We're here to see Alejandro," Randall said.

The maid's gaze flicked to the badge on Randall's uniform as if noticing it for the first time.

"Of course. I'll go get him."

Almost five minutes passed before the door opened again. Alejandro stood with his hands in his pockets. His dark eyes narrowed as he surveyed his three visitors. His gaze stopped on Kimber.

"Beth-Anne said you were here. I had to see it for myself. Now you can leave."

"Mr. De Costa, your daughter is here…"

"To advance her career, I bet. That's the only thing she cares about. A film where she investigates her own father would probably do gangbusters."

The thought had crossed her mind.

"She's here on official police business."

He gestured at the camera in Brunshea's hand. "That part of your official police business, Randall?"

"That's Sergeant Sykes, and yes. She's here as a consultant. We asked for her help, and we'd like to take a look at the crime scene."

"You can be my guest, Sergeant Sykes." Alejandro never stopped glaring at his daughter.

"They're both here in an official capacity, like I said."

Alejandro sniffed. He stared off in the distance. His jaw tightened.

"Fine. But the camera stays off."

Randall opened his mouth to protest.

"It's okay," Kimber said. "We don't need it."

"Well, she speaks," Alejandro said.

"Dad, I'm…"

"I don't want to hear it." His attention shifted to Randall. "You can take the footpath around the back of the house. You can show your way out when you're done."

Randall led the way to the back yard. Alejandro stared them down until they rounded the side of the house. They crossed the back yard into the thick foliage, where the path turned to gravel and crunched under their feet. The semen-like smell of

Callery Pear lingered in the air. Shade provided meager relief from the dank humidity. Kimber left Leonard seven years ago. She hated the summers most of all.

The vinyl shed stood at the edge of the woods. The door hung ajar. Some tools lay scattered on the concrete floor and in front of the structure.

"This is how the shed was left," Randall said. "Fingerprints came back to a few of your father's groundskeepers. He said none of them had been by since before Percy was killed. Rope from inside was used to tie the boy to the tree. Pruning shears were used to remove the boy's tongue. Also from the shed."

Kimber glanced back toward the house.

"Try and get some shots," she said to Brunshea.

"Now, Kimber, we have crime scene photos," Randall said. "Just use those. Don't want to add fuel to the fire."

"He's right," Brunshea said.

Kimber chewed her lip and nodded. She stepped forward, into the shed. The inside was in disarray.

"Whoever did this was in a rush," Kimber said.

"That's right."

She faced Randall and Brunshea. "This makes me think it wasn't premeditated at all. It was a crime of passion. Someone must have killed the boy in a fit of rage."

"The last person to see him alive was the man you're staying with. Henry said Percy knocked over one of his expensive cameras. Said he yelled at the boy, but didn't chase him. Not that I think Henry's in any shape to chase anybody."

"He's overweight. Besides, I see him caring more about salvaging the camera than chasing after someone who broke it."

"He said it was unsalvageable."

"Did he know that right away?"

Randall shrugged. Kimber stepped out of the shed and examined the lock.

"No sign of forced entry?"

"None, but your daddy said he lost the key a week and a half ago."

"His groundskeepers anyone I might know?" Kimber asked.

"Matter of fact, yes. Bruce Matteo works for your daddy

pretty regularly these days. Only started about six months ago, though. After he got sober."

Kimber nodded. She tried her damnedest to remain neutral. "Let's take a look at that tree, shall we?"

They resumed their trek. Brunshea caught up to Kimber's side.

"Hey," he said, keeping his voice low. "You okay?"

She ignored him. The mention of her ex-lover's name bit harder into her than she thought it would have. Brunshea said her name. She nodded, but remained silent, and kept on walking. They reached the edge of the creek and the end of her father's property. She stepped off the path, over undergrowth and jagged rocks. She stopped in a clearing, pressed her hand to a tree at its edge, an oak of enormous girth with half its branches shading the clearing and half its branches hanging over the creek.

"It was this tree, wasn't it?"

"The hell you know that?" Randall said.

"Curious about that myself," Brunshea muttered.

She walked around the tree's trunk, tracing patterns in the bark. She stopped at a carving: a heart with B.M. + K.D.C. engraved in its center. She shrugged, not wanting to tell them how she knew. *Because it's what I feared.*

"Kimber?" Brunshea said.

"This tree, this place, has significance for me." Kimber met Brunshea's gaze. "I'm sorry."

"What?"

"I lost my virginity right here in this clearing." She pointed to the initials B.M. "To Bruce Matteo."

"How bad was your breakup?" Randall asked.

"It was pretty ugly."

"Ugly enough for him to want to frame your father for murder?"

"I'm not sure. I don't put anything past anyone."

She stared at the initials and imagined Percy tied to the tree, writhing in agony.

"You didn't tell me," Kimber said when they got back to Henry's house.

"I beg your pardon?"

"You were the last person to see Percy alive."

"Except for the killer, whoever that may be."

"Did you see anything else?"

"I did not. I've already spoken with the police. I'll tell you what I told them: I was much too pissed off and focused on picking up the pieces of my camera to notice anything."

"I still wish you would have told me. I don't like things being kept from me."

Brunshea came out of the guest bedroom.

"Everything's put away. You sure you don't want to bring a camera with you?"

"Bruce won't talk to me if I film him. Of course, he may not talk to me at all."

"You just made all sorts of friends here."

"I left for a reason, same as you."

"Not all the same reasons."

His words hung for a five-count.

"I guess I can't argue there."

Brunshea shrugged. "Not everyone can relate."

"Are you sure you don't want one of us to go with you? You know, just in case he is dangerous?"

"I'll be fine," she said.

"Save it," Brunshea said. "I'll go with you."

"Really, it's not necessary."

"I wasn't asking."

"Suit yourself, but you're staying in the car."

Kimber parked in front of Bruce's house. She and Brunshea exchanged glances.

"If you're not out in an hour, I'm coming in," he said.

She slapped his chest. "Okay, tough guy."

They shared a laugh.

"Seriously though. Watch your ass in there."

"Noted."

Kimber got out of the car and walked up the path to the front door. She knocked and stepped back to wait for a response.

"Who is it?"

His voice made her belly clench. She opened her mouth to speak and could only produce a dry croak. She cleared her throat.

"It's Kimber."

The door flung open. The man on the other side of the doorway had a slouched posture, like unseen hands tugged at him, hoping to drag him down to some unfathomable darkness, like the act of standing made him weary. Streaks of gray shot through his once-black wavy locks. Three days' worth of beard stubble shadowed his cheeks. He wore a faded concert tee-shirt and blue jeans. Everything about him expressed a man beaten down. *Tired.* Kimber saw a man who had fallen many times, and managed to get up again and again, but had little fight left. The anger that had oozed through the phone in their final conversation had all but dried up. The man before her had lost all passion, and right away she could tell that he was no killer.

"Do you need a drink or anything?" Bruce asked.

Kimber's eyes flicked to the rows of empty bottles on the kitchen counter.

"Looks like you've had enough for the both of us, times about fifty."

He laughed. "Oh, those? I don't drink anymore. I keep those around to remind myself why. Trying to be better, you know?"

She couldn't decide whether or not to believe him. *It's not important. Just get the information you need. And try to ignore what you're feeling.*

What was she feeling? That's what made it so hard to ignore. She thought, at first, it might be pity, or maybe guilt. She had not spoken to or seen Bruce since her third semester at film school, almost eight years ago. She had started coming home less and less, immersed in her studies and trying to make short films of her own. Meeting Brunshea had further complicated things. The physical attraction was instant; their mutual love of film and true crime only deepened her affection for him. It was only a matter of time before she broke things off with Bruce.

You're a selfish bitch. A self-absorbed fucking bitch.

Maybe he was right, but not likely. Was it her fault he didn't share her passion for film? Or that he had no passion for anything other than tying her down when she got out of film school? Did that make her selfish? No, it just made him wrong for her.

But now, seeing him like this, she wanted to cry. She remembered the boy she used to go joyriding with through the winding, wooded roads of Tucker County, laughing and screaming and playing The Killers *Sam's Town* at full volume. She remembered the time they took each other's virginity, under the same tree where little Percy Wilkes bled to death, unable to speak, unable to scream. A sense of responsibility, however undeserved, came over her, and she wanted to hug him.

Stop it, Kimber. You've got a job to do.

Selfish bitch.

Stop it.

Self-absorbed fucking bitch.

"I'm glad you're doing better. I was actually hoping I could ask you some questions."

"About Percy?"

"How'd you know?"

"Lucky guess. Randall went to see you accept your reward in Sackettsville the week of Percy's death. I don't know. I thought maybe he might have asked for your help."

"You thought right."

Bruce nodded. "I saw Percy that day. I used to see him a lot. Used to hang out with the kid next door, Jordan. Then one day, he stopped coming around as much. That fucking kid used to hop the fence and eat my tomatoes, like a damn rabbit or some shit."

"Percy did?"

"Yeah. Anyway, that day, I heard some yelling next door. I came out to see what it was, and there's Percy, running down the street toward the woods. I wanted to go after him, but by the time I got my clothes on, he was gone."

"Tell me about the people next door."

"Jeffrey and Dory?"

"Jeffrey Watts? He and Dory got married?"

"Yeah. At least one couple from our graduating class stayed together."

"And Percy used to hang out with their kid?"

Bruce paused. His cheeks got pink as he realized his underhanded comment would go unacknowledged. He shook his head. "Yeah, and the other day, that was the first time I'd seen him over there in a really long time. Not sure exactly why they stopped hanging out, but I think someone got molested."

"Were you able to hear what they were yelling at Percy the other day?"

"Not really. Just... I don't know. Dory hasn't been in a good place. Maybe it has something to do with whatever happened between Percy and Jordan. Maybe not. I don't know. I heard they found him on your dad's property."

"I heard you've been working for my dad."

"Yeah, landscaping. It's a good gig."

"They found him at the tree."

"Which... oh, *that* tree."

"You had to think about it. I'm a little hurt."

Was she *flirting*?

He shrugged. "It's been a long time. I'm... Jesus, Kimber."

"What?"

"You think I fucking did it."

"Did I say that?"

"No, but fucking... don't pretend it hasn't crossed your mind."

"I can't leave any stone unturned. I just need to know what you know."

"I've told you all I know."

She stared hard at him. The air of the room was like a rubber band pulled taut, ready to snap.

"I believe you."

"You believe me?"

"I do."

"Just like that?"

"Just like that."

Kimber walked out of Bruce's house, but felt no relief. Night was falling. She needed to eat. She wanted to drink. She crossed the yard and cast a glance to the Watts residence. The boy, Jordan, stood in the lighted window, watching her. Her gaze drifted to the empty driveway. She wished the parents were home so she could question them, too.

She reached the car and slumped into the driver's seat.

"How'd it go?" Brunshea asked. The camera was on, recording her.

"He's not the killer."

"Just like that?"

"Just like that."

Henry had a movie projecting in his den. A droning synth score reverberated through the house, and Kimber guessed the film had been made in the late '70s or early '80s. When Kimber closed the door, he came into the living room.

"Everything go okay?" he asked. "You catch a killer?"

"Not yet."

"Ah, well, I just started Fulci's *Zombie.* You two want to join me?"

"I never understand how a man with a doctorate in film likes that Italian crap," Kimber said.

"That Italian crap is what made me want to get my doctorate in film."

"Fuck it, I'll give it a try," Brunshea said.

"You boys have fun. I'm going to take a shower."

She made her way to the guest bathroom and overheard Henry offering Brunshea a beer. She liked that they were getting along. Henry had been like a favorite uncle when she was in high school, had gotten her interested in film and lent him his equipment to shoot her first shorts. Later, after she and Alejandro had a falling out, she saw Henry as a surrogate father. Though she didn't expect her relationship with Brunshea to blossom into anything serious, she liked him better than any other man in her life, and wanted Henry to like him, too.

She showered and dressed in her pajamas and closed herself in the guest room. Something blinked on her phone, an email. The sender was a series of numbers at a domain name she didn't recognize. The email contained a single sentence and a video attachment.

The message: *You should leave.*

The attachment was too large to open on her phone, so she turned on her laptop. She scanned the attachment for viruses. Convinced the file was safe, she opened it. A grainy, VHS-quality video played. A boy wandered while his father chatted on a cell phone. The boy stood at the edge of a busy street. The father ended his phone call and ran for the boy. *Percy and his father. Has to be.*

The video ended. Her gaze flicked to the message.

You should leave.

Kimber grabbed her laptop and stomped into the den. The woman impaled eyeball-first on a splintered door brought a chorus of laughs from Henry and Brunshea.

"Hey, who all knows we're here?"

Henry paused the film. "Just Randall and me. Bruce and your father now, too, I suppose. Why?"

She told them about the email. She played the video for them.

"Apparently the killer knows now, too," Brunshea said.

"Shit, seriously?"

"Afraid so. We're just not equipped to trace that email here."

"Well, how long will State PD need it?"

"Wish I knew. You should probably turn it over though. Evidence and all."

"Right."

Kimber handed over the bag containing her laptop. Randall picked up the phone on his desk.

"Sergeant Sykes here. Need someone from evidence to come pick up a laptop. Need to trace an email. Right. Uh huh. Yeah, take care." Randall hung up. He returned his attention to Kimber. "They should be by this afternoon."

"They'll be careful, right? My whole life is on that fucking thing. I can't exactly afford to buy another one."

"You sure? You're an award-winning filmmaker."

"You'd think that'd make a difference, but no. There's a reason we're staying with Henry instead of getting a fancy hotel."

"Not that there are any fancy hotels in town."

"Well, right. There's that. Anyway, do you know anything about Percy molesting Jordan Watts?"

"Well, I heard rumors. Nothing concrete. Parents never came to us with anything."

"Still, I would like to talk with them. Bruce told me there was some kind of disturbance next door."

"Funny. Didn't say shit to us about it."

"No? Strange."

"Maybe it slipped his mind."

"Maybe." She stared into space, chewed her lip.

"What are you thinking?

She didn't want to tell him. She wondered if she was wrong about Bruce not being involved somehow, if her history with him somehow obscured her instincts. *He's too broken to be a killer, but maybe he knows more than he let on.*

"Nothing. I just don't know why he wouldn't have told you." She shook her head. "Either way, I'd like to talk to the Watts family. Maybe they can fill us in on more details of what happened that day."

Randall nodded. "Sounds good to me."

"What's up with Alejandro?"

"Your father is cooperating. He's agreed to stay in town and help us with whatever we need, assuming he doesn't have to see you again. Christ, Kimber, what happened with you two?"

"Nothing I feel like sharing. When can we see the Watts family?"

"Can go right now if you'd like. Don't have anything else on the agenda for the day."

Jeffrey Watts opened the door and narrowed his eyes at Randall and Kimber.

"Can I help you two?" He nodded at Randall. "Officer."

"We need to ask you some questions. About Percy."

Jeffrey cast a glance back into the house.

"Can it wait? Dory's not feeling well."

"Afraid it can't."

"Kimber, what are you doing in town?"

"I'm helping with the investigation."

"That's right," Randall said. "Anything you say to me, you can say in front of her."

"All right. Come on in. We have to be quiet though, Dory's sleeping. Have a seat. Excuse me for a minute."

Jeffrey walked to the back of the house. Muffled talking came from one of the bedrooms. Little Jordan walked out in front of his father. He gave Randall and Kimber a wave before walking outside to play.

"I don't want him to overhear. He'll get upset."

"Good call," Randall said. Jeffrey sat. Everyone stayed quiet for almost half a minute. "Heard there was a disturbance here, the day Percy went missing. Did Percy come by, try to see Jordan?"

"He did. We told him he had better leave."

Randall looked at his hands. He shifted and tried to think of what to say next.

"What happened to cause Jordan and Percy to stop hanging out?" Kimber asked.

Jeffrey eyed Randall for approval. Randall nodded.

"I, uh, well, something inappropriate. Something awful."

"Did Percy molest your kid?" Randall asked.

Jeffrey fixed his gaze on Randall. The corners of his eyes glistened. He didn't speak for a long time. Finally, he bit his lip and nodded.

"Christ, Jeffrey. Why didn't you come forward?"

"We handled it. There's no need to involve the police. They're..." He sighed. "...they're just kids."

"You should have come to us."

"I said, we handled it."

"How did you handle it?" Randall asked.

"We forbade them from seeing each other. Kept them apart. That's why we got so upset when Percy showed up the other day. I hate to think us turning him away led to his death though. He's... he wasn't a bad kid. Just troubled."

"How long has Dory been sick?" Kimber asked.

"Comes and goes."

"Did it start when Percy touched Jordan?"

His wet eyes locked onto her and hardened. "Just what are you getting at?"

"Nothing, I guess. Nothing yet."

He grimaced like he finished a shot of rotgut. Behind him, a door opened. Footsteps plodded down the hallway and into the living room. Dory stood in the doorway, her hair a mess of tangles, her eyes glazed and shadowed. Kimber couldn't tell if the woman was sick or hungover or both.

"I saw Bruce," she said and rolled back her shoulders. "He was following Percy up the street the day Percy came over."

"She's lying," Kimber said when they got back to the cruiser.

"How can you tell?"

"First, I didn't hear her get out of bed; she was waiting by the door for the right moment to jump into the conversation. Second, I used to be close with her. She always used to roll her shoulders when she was lying. It was some kind of nervous tick, like she wanted us to think she was standing up straight and facing us."

"Sounds like a hunch."

"You're right. We don't have a lot to go on. Also, if she's really that sick, she could be all out of sorts, not acting like herself, having her ticks go off at all the wrong times. I don't know. I don't think so." Kimber shook her head and checked her phone. "Shit."

"What?"

"I have twelve missed calls from Brunshea." She returned the calls. "Hey, what's going on?"

"Well, I did some research. You know your ex-boyfriend has a blog?"

"So, a lot of people have blogs."

"You should really see what he's been writing."

Back at Henry's house, Kimber read through Bruce's blogs, then she read them again. Henry had gone to the college for the day, and they had set up in the living room. Though no real names were used, the blogs were full of references to Kimber and how she broke his heart. The writings were fictional reflections on the relationship. What struck her most was how perfectly he captured her, every nuance, even moments she had forgotten. The most troubling line came from an entry dated three months ago.

She broke my fucking heart. I want to see her suffer. I want her to pay.

"That is some fucked up emo shit," Brunshea said.

"Revenge is more nu metal," Randall said.

Kimber glanced between them, shook her head and closed Brunshea's laptop.

"What are you thinking?" Brunshea asked.

"Between this, the initials on the tree, and Dory's testimony, it certainly looks like he's involved somehow."

Brunshea threw up his hands. "Involved somehow? Shit."

"You think maybe he killed Percy in hopes of luring you back home?"

"Far-fetched, but not impossible. Either way, it's still not enough to go on."

"Seems pretty obvious to me."

"No, she's right. I could bring him in for questioning. Maybe we could get a confession out of him."

Kimber nodded. "Okay."

"You don't seem like you're convinced," Brunshea said.

"He's not a killer. I just know it."

"Or you just don't want to go the rest of your life knowing you fucked a murderer."

"Or that."

"Kimber, sorry, I meant…"

"I think you said what you meant."

"All right, enough you two." Randall put a hand between them. "I'll take him in for questioning, see what I can find."

Kimber stood outside on Henry's back deck. A gentle breeze guided the trees in a delicate, swaying dance. Her hands gripped the railing. She had stood out here so many times as a teenager, shooting and acting in short films under Henry's guide. He was a friend of Kimber's mother and her parents trusted him with her. She stood out here now, thinking about what Brunshea said.

Or you just don't want to go the rest of your life knowing you fucked a murderer.

How fucked up had her life gotten that this was even a possibility? She still didn't think Bruce was involved, but as Brunshea's words echoed in her mind, she wondered if maybe some form of denial had worked its way inside her. It happened to people all the time. Mothers and wives lived day in and day out, unaware of the murderous doings of the men in their lives. Why should Kimber be any different?

Because I'm stronger. I'm better than that. Better than them.

I hope I'm right.

Kimber waited to hear back. She locked herself in the guest room, lay on the bed, and stared up at the ceiling. Waiting was not her style. Restlessness began with a clenching in her teeth. Soon, it spread to her shoulders and belly. The tension gripped every extremity. She got no call from Randall about Bruce. No word from the state police about her laptop. She got up and started pacing.

Brunshea knocked to bother her just once. He asked if she was okay.

"I'll be fine."

"Not what I asked," he said and walked away from the door.

She stopped pacing to check her email and her Twitter for the third time in ten minutes, something she did when nervous. She thought about calling Randall to check the status, but decided against it. Her thumb hovered over the screen of her phone. She opened her contacts and scrolled through. She found Bruce's number, a number she should have deleted long ago. Her breath caught like a dog at the end of its chain. She pressed the text message icon.

HEY. THINKING OF YOU. ARE YOU OKAY? REALLY OKAY?

What am I doing? This is stupid. Of all the stupid things I've done, this ranks really fucking high.

It was too late to take it back now. She set her phone in her lap and waited.

The response came less than a minute later.

NOT SO GOOD. SEEING YOU AGAIN REALLY THREW ME FOR A LOOP. I'VE MISSED YOU. HOW HAVE YOU BEEN?

She didn't know how to answer that. Everything looked good on the surface, even felt good. But like a scarred face repaired by plastic surgery, there were cracks beneath. She had no delusions of getting back with Bruce. They lived completely different lives. Nor did she have any desire to reconcile with him in a romantic way. She had moved on; he hadn't been right for her then, and wasn't right for her now. Closure, she did need. Bruce was only the first layer, a layer that didn't even contain her father. That was buried much deeper, though maybe not entirely unrelated. She had betrayed both men, and the memory of her mother, for the sake of her work.

Burying the hatchet with Bruce was only the beginning, a small step that she hoped would eventually lead to reconciling with her father. Of course, the timing was terrible. Bruce was now a suspect in a murder case, a murder case she was supposed to be helping the police solve.

Maybe I can help. If he's texting me, he hasn't been picked up yet. Maybe we can meet, and I can get him to confess.

She typed another message. WHERE ARE YOU?

BEEN DRIVING AROUND MOST OF THE AFTERNOON.

You're being stupid, Kimber. Don't do this.

DO YOU WANT TO MEET?

WHERE?

Stop messaging him now.

AT THE TREE.

Kimber entered the woods through the backway, avoiding Alejandro's property altogether. She used the flashlight on her phone. The darkness of the woods at night used to bring her comfort as a teenager. She used to go for late night walks, usually alone, but sometimes with Bruce. She enjoyed the crisp, earthy smells of leaves and dirt. She liked the cool breeze on her skin and how the leaves reminded her of whispering voices spreading torrid rumors.

Her feet plodded through the pine needles on the neglected path. This portion of the woods belonged to the town. Paying for maintenance of a trail was hard for a town the size of Leonard. Its small tax base meant such projects sometimes got neglected. Kimber thought it added a naturalism to an otherwise manmade path.

The pulse of the crickets thickened the air the farther she entered the woods. The sights, smells and sounds took her back.

The night she lost her virginity to Bruce they walked this path. She told Alejandro they were going to the movies. Bruce picked her up and drove her to the entrance of the woods. They brought two bottles of Old English with them and she downed almost a third of a forty in one pull to help loosen herself up. She had picked out the tree as an ideal place. One reason was the clearing, but the main reason was how it held special meaning for her. She would come to the tree all the time to sit and think throughout her teens. The place helped her clear her mind, and she hoped it, along with the alcohol, would help her get ready to have sex for the first time.

When they reached the clearing, they stood across from each other. A full minute passed without either of them saying anything. They only looked into each other's eyes.

"So," she said.

"So."

Bruce stepped forward and leaned in for a kiss. He stopped, inches from her face, and chewed his lip. It dawned on her then that he was as nervous as she was, and that made everything okay somehow. She reached up and took hold of the back of his neck. She got on her tiptoes and kissed him, soft on the lips. At the touch of her mouth, he fell into her. His tongue slipped inside her and they embraced.

They fumbled out of their clothes. Body heat radiated from Bruce and she clung to it, feeling a security she never felt her entire life. She let him kiss her neck and touch her breasts. She let him guide her to the forest floor, on the blanket they had spread. She closed her eyes when he entered her. A flash of pain gave way to bliss, completeness. She cried out and he asked if he hurt her and she said yes but that it was a good hurt.

She bit her lip until she could no longer stand the pain. She wanted so bad to push the memory away. She hurt somewhere inside, someplace fundamental and deep.

Kimber glanced around, suddenly paranoid, as if her reverie had made her vulnerable. To who or what she didn't know. She imagined an invisible mob of slut-shaming men who would make her pay for leaving Bruce the way she had. They would string her up and lash her with phallus-shaped whips. They would double their efforts when they learned of how she didn't attend her mother's funeral. The violence wouldn't stop until her body simply gave up.

Maybe I am bad. Maybe I do deserve to be punished.

No, I don't.

Of course, whether she deserved it or not wouldn't matter. Not to those who wished to see her punished.

Maybe coming out here was a bad idea. She thought about the journals and their violent language. *It was definitely a bad idea. What the hell was I thinking?*

She came to the clearing, stared up at the tree where Percy Wilkes had died. Ghosts had filled these woods long before Percy's death. She used the flashlight to check the ground for bugs but decided not to sit. If Bruce did get violent, if she was wrong about him, she didn't want to be prone. Kimber stood in the middle of the clearing and waited.

Bruce never came. Kimber waited an hour before she called Brunshea.

"Girl, where'd you go?"

She took a breath and contemplated not telling him. He would think she was crazy, and she would agree with him. Nothing good would come of telling him. Of course, she had disappeared without telling anyone. He had to know something was up. She needed to have *some* sort of explanation. She decided to tell him.

"You're right. I do think you're crazy. Glad you're okay though. He never showed, huh?"

"No."

"You should get back. It's been a long day."

"I... yeah. Yeah." She shook her head, wanted nothing more than to lie down, to sleep for days. "Do you know if Randall was able to find him?"

"No one's been able to find him, which is exactly why you need to get your ass back here."

"Yeah, okay." She hated taking direction from anyone, but felt too weak to say no. "I'll be back soon.

She got back and let Brunshea and Henry scold her for running off. Then she went to bed. She kept the room dark, but didn't sleep. She thought about her trip to the woods, and her reasons for it. Maybe Bruce was a lost cause. Her father might prove more receptive. She resolved to call him in the morning, but didn't sleep any better because of it.

Kimber and her father met for breakfast at a diner called The Gathering, a place Kimber used to spend many nights drinking coffee with her friends and talking about her dreams of working in film. Her father looked around before he sat down.

"Huh, no cameras?"

"I meant what I said, Dad. I'm trying to make an effort, okay? I know I fucked up."

"There's a first."

"Come on. Can't we just have breakfast?"

"First, I want you to promise me something."

"What?"

"I want you to come to the grave with me before you leave. Can you promise me you'll do that?"

"Sure. Of course." She nodded. "I promise."

They finished their meals. She got up to leave. They hugged. It was stiff and strange.

Her phone rang on her way to her car. Brunshea.

"Hello?"

"Kimber. It's Bruce."

"What about him?"

"They found him underneath a bridge. He jumped. He's dead."

"Case closed," Randall had said. Bruce killed himself because of guilt. Because he sensed Kimber closing in on him.

"I don't know. Something about this doesn't feel right."

Brunshea had the camera on her. They were sitting on Henry's porch, just the two of them after Randall made his declaration that the case was closed. Henry was in his viewing room watching another Italian zombie flick. Kimber stared at her hands, couldn't bring herself to look at the camera lens. At the end of each case, they always did an interview.

"Sometimes life doesn't feel right, Kimber. Sometimes it's all random, you know?"

"Are you trying to make me feel better? I hope you're not, because you're doing a terrible job."

"No, I'm just… Do you want to do this later? I can turn the camera off."

"Let it roll. I want to go on record saying this isn't over."

"Kimber…"

"No, listen, Brunshea. I came here to solve a case and that's what I'm going to do."

"What case did you come here to solve, Kimber?"

"He's not a killer. He may have killed himself, but he's not a killer. He didn't murder Percy."

"What are you thinking?"

"I'm still hung up on Dory. She lied and I don't like the history with their son and Percy. I think they have more motive than anyone else."

"Sure, but I don't know. I mean, there's the video, which seemed to target you specifically. Only Bruce would do something like that. I mean, you read his blogs."

"I did, but that doesn't necessarily mean much. The last entry was almost four months ago. Maybe he was telling the truth; he's been healing."

"Maybe being the star killer of one of your cases is how he healed."

"I don't know."

"Look, I'm not gonna get jealous if you still have feelings for Bruce. Not like we're exclusive."

"Who are you seeing? You spend all your time with me."

"No one, but I'm saying, we ain't married or anything."

"Sometimes I feel like we are."

He laughed. She laughed. Neither sounded humorous.

Brunshea shut off the camera.

"Maybe we should finish this interview later."

Kimber nodded. Brunshea got up to go inside.

"Brunshea." He stopped in his tracks. "Bruce didn't have my private email address."

"So?"

"The video came to my private email address."

"No way he could have gotten it?"

"I doubt it."

Brunshea shook his head. "Look, I'm headed to sleep. You should sleep, too. You got a lot on your plate."

"I'll be in in a minute."

Brunshea waited, then nodded and walked back inside.

Kimber waited until everyone fell asleep. She recalled her meal with her father. When he had gotten up, she had glimpsed his keys. One of them was marked *Shed*. He told Randall he had lost his key to the shed. That was part of his alibi.

Kimber got to her feet. She walked out to her car and started it. She drove back to her father's house. He answered the door after several knocks drew him out of bed. He examined her with a bleary-eyed gaze.

"Kimber."

"Can I see your keys, Dad?"

"What for?"

"Your keys."

"Christ, Kimber." He handed her his keys. "Now, what…"

She took off down the footpath. He called after her. She came to the edge of the woods and marched to the shed. She tried the key in the lock. It opened. She spun to face her father who was chasing after her.

"What is this, Kimber?"

"You said you lost this key?" she said, holding it up to him.

"Yeah, I found it. So what?"

"So what? A fucking murder was committed with tools from your shed and all you have to say is *so what*?"

His features went hard. "You better watch your tone. After we had a nice breakfast, you have the fucking nuts to come to my house and accuse me of murder?"

"First, I'm your daughter. I don't have nuts. Second, I need to make sure no stone is unturned. My... Bruce killed himself tonight. Everyone thinks he's Percy's killer."

"Maybe he is."

"No, Dad. I know he's not. The killer sent me a video to my private email. He never had my private email. You did though."

"Me and who else? Do you really think I killed that little retard?"

"He's not... why do I even bother?"

"I'm wondering the same thing. You need to get the hell out of here."

"Maybe, but you need to come with me."

"You don't get it, Kimber. You need to get off my property, or I'm going to shoot you."

"You'd shoot your own daughter?"

"You're not my daughter. You've done nothing but turn your back on what's left of this family."

Kimber stared at her father. He stared right back. It was a duel without a gun, unless of course Alejandro really meant to shoot her. Finally, he dropped his gaze.

"Please go," he said. "I can't stand to look at you right now."

Kimber stormed back to her car.

Kimber drove without aim for almost two hours. She kept the music up and tried to silence her thoughts. The break in her dad's voice, as he told her he couldn't stand to look at her, bothered her more than his threats to shoot her. She had never known her father to be a weak man. Always authoritative and strong in his convictions, he now came off as a man reduced and degraded, a dried-up husk inside which a strong and proud man once lived. She hated seeing him like that. She hated herself for making him like that.

And it was me that made him that way. I should have been there for him when mom died. I should have put Bruce and all these petty reasons why I didn't want to go home behind me. I should have been a better daughter.

Kimber ended up at the Last Call Pub, several blocks from

Henry's home. She glanced at the car radio. Two and a half hours until closing time. She went inside and sat down. The Last Call was the only bar in town that still allowed smoking. It served no food. No fancy craft beers, not unless Corona counted. She ordered a shot of Jack and a bottle of Moosehead. She pounded the shot of Jack in one gulp and chased it with two swigs of beer. She surveyed her surroundings, her gaze stopping on a familiar face.

Jeffrey Watts sat on the other end of the bar, staring forlornly into a bottle of Yuengling. She picked up her beer and approached him. She sat down. He looked at her and blinked. Judging by the redness in his eyes, she guessed the beer was his fifth or sixth.

"Shouldn't you be taking care of your wife?" she asked.

"Sometimes a man needs a break. Shouldn't you be off solving the crime of the century?"

"Sometimes a lady needs a break."

"Guess we had the same idea," he said and raised his drink. "Anyway, Dory can be difficult. She's an alcoholic. Been drinking herself into a stupor damn near every day since Percy touched Jordan. Oh, and the irony isn't lost on me. Drinking to take the edge off of dealing with an alcoholic wife."

"Do I look like I'm judging?" Kimber pounded more of the beer and ordered herself a second round. "Whatever he wants, too."

Jeffrey ordered another lager. They sat in silence. Kimber pounded another shot, finished her first beer and got halfway into her second.

"Hey, I've seen your films. Glad one of us made it."

"Nothing's stopping you from taking it up now."

"Aw, it's too late. Besides, I'm out of practice. I haven't held a camera since community college. That documentary we did on campus rape."

"You know, it wasn't *that* long ago."

"Feels like ages. I've missed you Kimber. Hell, everyone missed you. Wish you would've just come back on your own."

"I couldn't. Didn't even want to come back this time to tell you the truth." She shook her head. "Dad and I are probably never going to talk again now."

"That sucks. I'm sorry. I heard about Bruce. I'm sorry about that, too."

He was slurring. She regretted buying him another round, but the damage was done. Too late to worry now.

"Thank you. Hey, you're not driving are you?"

"No, ma'am. Walking my ass home."

"Yeah, well, stay out of the road, okay? You don't want to stumble."

Kimber got up, wished him well, and walked back outside. She got in her car and drove slowly back toward Henry's. Once inside, she crashed on the couch, her conversation with Jeffrey playing on a loop in her mind.

The phone woke Kimber from a dead sleep. She felt around for it and almost ignored the call, but Randall's name on the screen changed her mind. She answered.

"Christ, Kimber. You sound like hell."

"I feel like it. What's up?"

"Where's Henry?"

She sat up, rubbed the back of her neck. "I don't know. Why?"

"Well, the state police traced that email. The IP comes back to him. He must have sent the video."

"But that's impossible." Silence on the line. "I mean, it's Henry."

"Nonetheless, I'll be over shortly. Need to take him in for questioning."

"Right." They disconnected the call. Someone knocked on her door. "Yeah?"

"It's Brunshea. You up?"

"I'm getting there."

"Henry's making breakfast."

Henry. Henry, who might be led away in cuffs within the next half hour.

"Okay. I'll be right there."

She came to the table. The bacon and eggs smelled great to her hungover self.

"Morning, sunshine," Brunshea said.

"Eat a dick," Kimber said.

Henry laughed. It was a goodhearted, jolly sound. Guilt overcame Kimber. This man had taught her everything she knew. If not for him, she never would have pursued film so intensely. Working with him as a teenager had inspired and informed her. It killed her to know the police were coming and not being able to warn him. *If he's guilty, he deserves no sympathy.* The words rang hollow. She wanted to help him. Most of all, she hoped to God he wasn't guilty, that this was all some sort of misunderstanding. Despite the pangs in her gut, she couldn't eat the delicious food set in front of her. She poked at it with her fork.

"You good?" Brunshea said.

"Yeah, just hungover."

"You went drinking?"

"Yeah."

"I don't blame her," Henry said. "It's been a tough few days."

"Should have invited me is all," Brunshea said.

"I needed to be alone."

"Did you watch your ass? Just in case Bruce wasn't our guy, I mean."

Kimber glanced down at her food. It crossed her mind that Henry could have poisoned her if he wanted. *Get a grip, Kimber. Just eat. You'll be fine. He'll be fine. Everything will be fine.*

But nothing was fine. Bruce was dead and a primary murder suspect. She never got any measure of closure from him. Her father hated her. Her head hurt like a bitch.

Selfish bitch. Self-absorbed fucking bitch.

"I think I need to lie back down," she said.

Brunshea and Henry exchanged glances. Henry nodded.

"Sorry you didn't like the food."

"It's not that, I'm just..."

"Hungover," Brunshea said. "Got it."

Kimber pushed away from the table just as there was a firm knock on the door.

"Who do you suppose that is?" Henry asked.

Kimber kept her mouth shut. Henry went to answer the door and she watched, acid burning in her gut and creeping up her esophagus. Randall and another patrol officer stood in the door as it swung open.

"Officers. How can I be of assistance?" Henry asked.

"You can come with us," Randall said.

"Come with you? What for? I've already told you all I know about Percy."

"This isn't a request, Henry."

Kimber put her head down.

"Officers, Randall, I assure you…"

"Save it. You have the right to remain silent. Might want to exercise that about now."

They led him away without another word.

Kimber kept her head down, peering into her now-cold eggs and bacon. Warmth closed around her hand. She glanced up to face Brunshea. He examined her, his dark eyes soft.

"You knew, didn't you?" he said.

"It's not right. It's not him."

"Kimber," he began, his tone sharp as if he meant to argue with her. He sighed. "Well, you were right about Bruce. Maybe you'll be right about Henry."

Kimber pulled her hand away, folded it in her lap. She focused on the pain of the hangover. She hadn't gotten drunk in almost a year—at a wrap party—and her body was not taking it well. There was a burn in her stomach and an ache in her side. Her head felt like it was being squeezed by an Olympic weightlifter.

Her thoughts drifted back to the previous night. The conversation with Jeffrey reverberated in her mind again.

"How did he know?" she said.

"What?"

She shook her head. She told Brunshea how she ran into Jeffrey Watts at the bar.

"He knew Bruce was dead. How the hell did he know Bruce was dead? The only way he could have known was if he was involved. It wasn't public knowledge yet. I need you to mic me."

"What?"

"Mic me up. I'm going over there and I'm getting a confession."

Brunshea opened his mouth to protest and closed it a second later. He knew better than to argue with her when she had her heart set on something.

"I'm going with you, if what you say is right. I'll wait in the car and…"

"…and if I'm not out in an hour, you break down the fucking door."

"Look at us. Finishing each other's sentences. I guess we are married."

She kissed him on the corner of the mouth. "Mic me."

When she knocked, no one answered. She waited and knocked again. A childish voice asked, "Who is it?"

"It's Kimber De Costa. I'm a friend of your parents. Are they home?"

A pause. "No."

"Can I come in and talk to you?"

Another pause. "My parents say I'm not supposed to let in strangers."

Smart boy. "I just want to talk. About Percy."

Another pause, this one a lot longer.

"And I'm not a stranger. Like I said, I'm a friend of your parents."

The silence continued. Kimber prepared to give up. She turned. Brunshea shrugged at her behind the wheel of their car. She took one step off the porch, and the front door to the house opened. A little boy stepped out. Jordan.

"What do you want?" he asked.

"Can I come inside?"

Jordan turned away. He pushed the door closed behind him. Kimber stepped forward and pushed the door back open. Jordan stopped in the center of the living room and faced her. Kimber stepped inside. A door opened in the hallway. Dory stepped out. She didn't look drunk or hungover or sick.

"Kimber," Dory said.

Kimber nodded at her old friend. "Your son was just about to tell me about Percy."

"Daddy made sure Percy couldn't hurt me anymore."

Kimber kept her eyes on Dory. "That's right. He and your mom sent him away. And he's never coming back. Is he?"

Jordan shook his head. Dory's lip quivered.

The police found Henry's computer, loaned to Jeffrey and Dory Watts, at the Watts residence. Jeffrey got home while the police were arresting Dory. He broke down and confessed to sending the video, to covering for Dory after she killed Percy, to pushing Bruce from the bridge. It was all a lot messier than Kimber would have liked. She had hoped to spare Jordan the sight of watching his parents get taken away in handcuffs.

"You good?" Brunshea asked Kimber while they sat in their car, after the police drove away with the Watts family.

"Not really."

"Wanna leave?"

She nodded. "Yeah. Definitely."

"Need to do anything in town before we do?"

She thought about seeing her father. She thought about her mother's grave at Fairview Cemetery, still never seen by her. Her father had threatened to shoot her, right after she accused him of murder. She didn't feel much like telling that story to her mother's headstone, even if her mother couldn't hear her.

"No," she said. "Let's just go."

Brunshea started the car. They went.

Waters of Ruin

It began with the poem. Fern found the typewritten pages in an envelope the weekend after her mother died. Every year, on the anniversary, she spread them across her bed and tried to make sense of them. Now, the summer before starting community college, she believed the verses held some great secret. Sometimes she thought the poem was nonsense and considered throwing it in the garbage. Other times she thought it was the most profound piece of work in the history of the written word.

The edges of the sheets had creased and crinkled. She had three notebooks filled with her musings on the poem, sketches drawn from the imagery, and copied verses with keywords circled. A fourth notebook sat beside her, half the pages already filled.

The poem was all Fern had left of her mother. There were pictures around the house, sure, but anyone could smile for a camera. Such portraits showed so little of one's true self.

The anniversary was the only day she allowed herself to grieve and explore the poem. The other three hundred and sixty-four days a year, she still spent most of her time reading, but not the poem. Instead she preferred indie press authors like Nate Southard, Tiffany Scandal, and Rios de la Luz. Some of these authors she'd even had the pleasure of meeting at conventions. Despite her interest in books, she had no literary aspirations herself. She wanted to be a doctor. A psychiatrist, specifically.

Fern dropped the pen in the middle of transcribing and sighed. She stretched her fingers and covered her eyes. In the darkness, she wondered if it was dark where her mother was, if her mother was anywhere at all. She didn't think about this all the time, but on the anniversary, she couldn't help herself. Julie had invited her to a party at a friend's house, but Fern couldn't bring herself to accept. As badly as she wanted to see Julie, the timing was all wrong. It hurt her that Julie had forgotten tonight was the anniversary, but she would forgive it, as she forgave everything Julie did. Fern could never stay angry with her. They had too much history; Fern loved her too much. Forgiving Julie came easily; forgetting the ache she caused did not.

Fern got up, left the pages spread about like pieces of an unsolvable puzzle.

Downstairs, she filled the coffeemaker with water. Her father sat at the dinner table holding a bottle of Miller High Life and staring at a full plate of reheated chicken lo mein. He still wore his black suit, but his tie hung loose, the top two buttons of his shirt undone. She had her ritual on the anniversary, and he had his. Judging by the time of night and the glassy stare of his eyes, Fern guessed the beer was his third or fourth. He would say he planned to "have a beer for your mother," but he always had more than that.

"How are you holding up?" she said.

He raised his bottle and shrugged.

"Just remember to eat something. We don't want a repeat of last year."

Last year, he had killed eight bottles of High Life, and Fern had to undress him and put him to bed.

He gave a smile that looked like it hurt and she had to turn away. She loaded a K-Cup and hit 'Brew.'

"Did you get a chance to visit her grave?" she asked.

"Put some flowers on it. She always fucking hated flowers."

"It's the best we can do."

He took a swig of beer.

"I'm going back upstairs." She kissed his forehead. "Eat something."

Her phone beeped in her room. She maintained her pace up the stairs, keeping a firm grip on the full coffee mug. The phone beeped again when she entered. She checked it. Two messages from Julie.

FERN, ARE YOU THERE? Then, I NEED YOU TO COME GET ME.

Fern glanced at the pages spread across her sheets and the notebook open on a page of her scrawl. She typed a response: SUP? EVERYTHING K?

NO, PLZ JUST GET OVER HERE. GUYS STARTING TO SCARE ME.

Fern put on her flashers and left her car in the street. She ran up to the front door of the party house and jabbed the doorbell. Commotion filled the inside, drunken shouting and throbbing bass. She hammered on the door.

A boy Fern's age opened the door. He wore plaid shorts and a shirt emblazoned with the logo of a band Fern had never heard of. He gnashed a wad of gum between his teeth.

"Something I can help you with, sweetie?"

"Where's Julie?"

"Julie? Dunno her. Maybe try the next house."

She shoved past him. He stumbled and fell on his ass. Several people crowding the front room noticed and erupted into laughter. Fern pushed through them, scanned the room for Julie. The people packed the room, drowning in each other's company. Fern had never liked parties.

Fern didn't see Julie in any of the first-floor rooms, so she went upstairs, past a boy who sat with his face in his hands and a puddle of vomit steaming between his shoes. She clawed her way through a line of people holding beers. A voice behind her said, "Bitch pushed right past me."

She opened the first bedroom doors. A couple in their underwear groped each other like they'd never get another chance. Somewhere, Julie screamed. Fern scrambled down the hallway toward the cry. Grabbed the doorknob on one of the other bedrooms. Locked. Shit.

"Open the door."

"Fernie? Oh God, Fernie. Help."

"Shut the fuck up." A male voice.

"That's her." A voice down the hall, the boy from the front door. Two other guys with him.

Fern slammed her shoulder into the door.

"Occupied." The male from inside.

"Open up, goddamn it."

"Fuck off."

The guy from the door and his friends drew closer. Fern kicked at the bedroom door, remembering how her father had kicked at the bathroom door the night her mother died. The door gave way and Fern stumbled inside. Someone tried to grab her, but she thrust back an elbow. Soft tissue gave way.

Julie stood across the bed in her bra and panties. She held a broken beer bottle in front of her like a gun. Fizz dripped from the glistening, jagged tips. A bulky guy with bleach-blond hair stood holding his genitals in his hand. He spun and faced Fern.

"What the…"

"Fucking bitch broke my nose," his friend said.

"Let Julie go."

The guy from the door and his two friends came inside. One of them said, "Uhhh…."

"You going to let her go, or do you want everyone in this house to know how small your cock is?"

Broken Nose Guy whimpered. The boy holding his genitals pulled his pants up and stepped aside. Julie sobbed and dropped the bottle. Fern crossed the room and wrapped her friend in one of the bedsheets. Together they descended the stairs, through the sea of people and out into the night.

Fern helped Julie into her dark house. Her father had made it to bed. Good. She didn't want to carry two drunks up the stairs tonight.

In Fern's room, Julie slumped bleary-eyed onto the edge of the bed. The sheet fell off her shoulders, exposing her tight body. The top half of her left nipple peeked above her black bra. Fern went to the closet and came back with yoga pants and a white top.

"You can sleep in this. You'll be a lot more comfortable."

Julie tossed the clothes aside and took hold of Fern's wrists. "Come here."

"Jules…"

"It's okay," Julie pulled her close. "I want to be with you tonight."

"You won't feel that way tomorrow."

Julie shrugged. "Come on, Fernie. Just forget about tomorrow for once."

Fern tried to pull away, torn between wanting a blissful night with Julie and fearing that by morning it would wash away like a dream. Julie tightened her grip on Fern's wrists and lay back, guiding Fern into a sloppy embrace. The full contact made Fern's desires impossible to resist. They kissed, Julie's mouth working sloppily on Fern's. Fern tried to control it, to approach the kiss delicately, but Julie's drunken passion released five years' worth of infatuation. She ran her fingers through Julie's blonde locks, pulled her lips from Julie's mouth, and sucked the soft skin of Julie's neck. Her friend's moans of pleasure encouraged her affection. She reached down between Julie's legs and touched the wetness there.

Julie wailed with pleasure. In fear of waking her father, Fern pressed her free hand against Julie's lips. Julie kissed and sucked on their tips. Fern tugged down Julie's panties and lowered her face into her friend's glistening sex. A rush of revelatory passion and cosmic fulfillment overcame her. All anxiety disappeared. Thoughts of her mother and the confusing poem she left behind disappeared. When they finished, they lay in each other's arms, and Fern dreamed of wandering in waist-deep water, searching for something she couldn't define.

Fern opened the door to the Crenshaw Mansion. A long, dark hallway stretched before her, terminating at a crossroads where another hallway could take her either to the right or the left.

Fern recited the words of the poem in her head as she took tentative steps forward. She marveled at how tragic and compelling it remained. Fern could only hope that her own personal tragedies could result in such a legacy.

Fern walked down the hallway. Though the wood floor had been restored recently, it still creaked as if it was old. The artwork on the wall appeared to be medieval woodcuts of mythical imagery: snakes curling around trees, alchemists holding flasks full of strange formulas, horned devils and nude nymphs, animals frolicking in lush wilderness. From the ceiling, chandeliers hung from wrought-iron hooks.

At the crossroads, a draft blew in from outside, raising gooseflesh on her skin. She stood there, trying to assess which way to go. The draft blew again and she turned back to the front door, thinking maybe she left it open, or Julie had decided to follow her in, but it was tightly shut.

Ten paces down the left path, a brass chain barricaded the walkway. She unhooked it. She stepped into the forbidden section and reattached the chain behind her. Ahead the hallway opened up to a massive parlor, decorated with old antique furniture. She imagined that each piece had its own story, from the grand piano to the bulky lounge to the animal-skin carpet.

Entering the openness of the parlor, she expected to lose the claustrophobia of the hallway, but the atmosphere of the place remained oppressive, like she stepped into a room full of ghosts.

A staircase spiraled up into an unseen loft. Heavy drapes covered the windows. Water ran somewhere below in one of the town's underground channels. There were entire histories written about these channels, their construction, their purpose; they were her town's claim to fame.

She proceeded across the parlor to the piano and lifted the fall-board to reveal keys stained with age and dirt. She tapped an out-of-tune melody. It came out close to coherent, but the instrument hadn't been tuned in years, maybe even decades. Still, touching it was like getting to know it somehow.

Somewhere a door slammed and she jumped to her feet.

Someone screamed and she thought, *Julie.*

She turned and bolted back toward the hallway, heart pounding. Julie screamed again and it was filled with terror. She bounded to the brass chain and tried to unhook it, but it slipped from her hands.

"Fern, help!" Julie called.

Fern fiddled with the chain, but couldn't seem to get it loosened. She leapt over it instead. As she ran, the floorboards groaned like infirm patients. Water seeped up from the seams and splashed beneath her feet.

She passed through the hall of arcane woodcuts, the works' subjects eyeing her with judgment. She slammed into the door and tried to force it open. Julie's screams became muffled, by distance or by someone placing a hand over her mouth. Fern kicked the door open and vaulted down the front steps. She froze.

A red-skinned imp held Julie in its arms. Three large horns spiraled from its head and waving tendrils whipped out behind its body like so many tails. Black eyes bored into Fern. Julie stared at Fern, too, her eyes stricken with dread. A groan like an out-of-tune piano emitted from the beast, and Fern thought it might be its breath.

Its body shredded open, exposing pulsing red organs and yellow fat tissue. The skin flaps enwrapped Julie and pulled her into the creature's body. The imp melted into a red blob, Julie screaming without sound beneath the rubbery flesh. The blob slinked away like an obese inchworm. It entered the house and disappeared between its doors.

Hopelessness washed over Fern, much like when she found her mother in the bathtub.

Then she heard Julie again. Screaming.

The hallway had changed. The hanging chandeliers now shined crimson light and cast fiery shadows upon the woodcuts, making the pictures bleed black. Shallow water sloshed under every step Fern took.

Now, alone in the house, her heart ached as she remembered Julie, the blonde little girl that used to play in the sandbox with her during recess; the awkward teenager whose only escape from the cruelty of others and her changing body was within her sketchbook; the kiss they shared at age eleven and never told a soul; and Julie the grown-up, curvy blonde for whom Fern still pined. All those beautiful pictures of her friend disappeared, as if someone had shut off a video stream, when Julie screamed again.

She couldn't pinpoint the exact location of the cries. They seemed to come from all around her.

I hear your scream in every gust of wind, in every sad love song, in every mournful howl of dogs abandoned and chained.

The shadows shifted to reveal a staircase as she recited the words. She recognized the stairs' faded cherry finish. The teeth marks from where her dog Blake liked to chew reminded her of a more innocent time. They belonged to her childhood home.

She came to the foot of the stairs. Above her the last few steps at the top built themselves, growing out of the darkness like strange fungus before solidifying into the cherry wood.

She ascended into the dark. At the top, she flicked on the light and illuminated a hallway that stretched to the right. Thirteen-year-old Fern, with her heart-printed white shorts and matching night shirt stood at the door to the bathroom, and nineteen-year-old Fern knew what night it was.

"Mom," the younger Fern said, and knocked.

Footsteps rushed up behind the older Fern and her father ran past her, oblivious to her. He put a hand on the younger Fern's shoulder and said, "What's going on, sweetie?"

"Mom's been in there a long time, over an hour, so I'm trying to check on her, but she's not answering."

"She probably has her headphones in."

Young Fern held up her mother's iPod. Her father's face wrinkled with worry. He knocked firmly on the bathroom door.

"Diana! You okay in there?"

No response.

Little Fern began to cry, and older Fern joined her. This was the defining moment of her life. Her obsession with Ruin began here. Her mother's note said everything was Ruined—she capitalized the 'R.' Fern discovered the poem not long after, discovering a kindred spirit in suffering.

"Losing her was terrible," her father said, his voice like ice. "I never expected to lose you, too."

Fern's breath caught in her throat. Her father's last statement stuck in her like an arrow to the heart. She stumbled back, nauseous and dizzy. A fear deeper than any chamber below this mansion welled up inside her.

"No," she whispered, unable to muster the strength to say it any other way. "No, no, no."

"Yes," he said. "I lost you, too."

Your loss is water in my lungs.

Water gushed from the bathroom, destroying the door and washing over thirteen-year-old Fern and her father, turning them to statues of wet sand and carrying them away. The water gave off a mucky smell, like earth soaked from days of rain. The wave crashed against the opposite wall, leaving water to pool across the hallway floor. She backed away, afraid to let it touch her.

The water stopped pouring from the room, as if someone shut off a valve somewhere, but it continued sloshing down the hallway, in an ankle-deep pool. Inside the bathroom, a voice, croaking and weak.

"Here, here, here," it said. "You can only come this way."

It repeated those words like a mantra and the more Fern listened, the more it sounded like her mother, a voice she still remembered, six years after the suicide. It was in a tone her mother used when she was tired, a tone Fern heard all too often. Her mother had been loving, but often seemed sad and aloof. Fern thought, not for the first time, that she should've known her mother was crying for help.

"You can only come this way."

Fern proceeded, stepping into the filthy water. As it soaked through her shoes, it stung her skin like corrosive chemicals. She shut her eyes as she reached the bathroom door, afraid of what waited inside.

"Fern," the voice said.

Fern opened her eyes. Her mother stood beside the bathtub in a white robe. Her dark hair was messy and she wore a tired smile, but she was alive. She held out her skinny arms, urging Fern to enter them, to embrace her.

"Please, sweetie. I've missed you so, so much."

Fresh tears streamed down Fern's cheeks. She sloshed through the water and caught a look at herself in the mirror above the sink. She too looked alive. She couldn't be dead. There was no way.

"Come to me," her mother said. "It's okay. I'll help you find your way."

She collapsed into her mother's arms and they squeezed

each other. Her mother fell back, taking Fern with her, into the bathtub, under the water. It was warm and soothing, not like the puddles in the hallway.

A muffled splash filled Fern's ears as she and her mother sank into water too deep for the tub. She hugged her mother more tightly and the affection was returned. The water got darker, but it maintained its soothing warmth.

I can stay here forever. If I am dead and this is where I'm bound to stay, I can do this. I can do this.

Julie cried out, tugging Fern out of her reverie.

No, please.

"Fern! Help me!"

The cries came from above. The bathroom light faintly glowed above, like the sun above the sea.

"Fern!" Julie called.

Fern looked at her mother for guidance, but saw the dead face of a drowned woman, the face she broke through her father's restraints to observe. The dead woman held her in a rigor mortis grip. Fern struggled, the embrace now filling her with panic, as they sank deeper and Julie's cries grew more distant.

Her mother's body decomposed before her, falling apart like it was made of cheap paper. She was willing it to fall apart, realizing as she lay clutched in the dead woman's embrace that her mother's death had been an anchor for her since it happened, weighing her down and preventing her from coming into her own.

Fern broke free and swam to the surface. Her face broke through the water and she sucked in a lungful of air.

She stepped out of the tub and searched for a way out. The door had disappeared. She walked over to the vanity and ducked to open the cabinet. No exit, just wood panels and some pipes.

Fern rose to her feet and looked in the mirror at her dirty, soaking reflection.

She glanced back at the tub. Its waters had darkened with blood, and the surface bubbled.

She glanced back at her reflection. She was stuck, her

newfound triumph over old wounds slipping away.

Then her reflection reached for her. Its hand passed through the mirror glass like it was reaching out of water and opened its palm. Fern jumped back against the wall. She looked down at the extended hand, then back at her reflection.

The wall in the mirror's frame melted away and gave way to darkness, but the wall behind Fern stayed solid. Julie's scream echoed, somewhere out in the deep. Fern's reflection faced her again.

The reflection nodded down at its extended hand. Fern looked down at it. She reached out. The hand was cold and wet, like hers. Fern's reflection pulled her into the mirror and the dark beyond.

Fern crawled through a mucky hole. Up ahead, more darkness waited. Her reflection was gone. She twisted her body through tight crevices, sucked in precious breath. Her hands fumbled in front of her for something to hold. The Waters of Ruin sloshed in the darkness below.

When she reached the end of the tunnel, she lowered herself, but her feet met no surface. As she hoisted her body up, a red light burst below her, illuminating a vast cavern. A rocky surface lay not far from her feet. Beside the bank, the gushing Waters of Ruin splashed against the stone embankments. Stalactites and stalagmites stuck out like jagged teeth, ready to chomp down upon anyone wandering the cavern. She lowered herself inside and scanned her surroundings for Julie and the red imp.

She proceeded along the bank, around jutting rocks and pits to even deeper caverns. Guided by red light, she came upon an empty noose. A red hand clutched the empty noose. The rope swung in the chilly underground air. The imp stood above her, atop a crag of rock.

"Where's Julie?" she asked.

His mouth spread into something like a grin. Fern stepped forward. She asked again where Julie was and the imp cocked his head to the side.

Fern glanced around for a sharp rock. When she found one, she hoisted it and stepped forward. "You think I'm fucking around?" She stopped when she saw Julie, up to her calves in the Ruin, sinking in slow motion with a blank expression on her face. "Julie!"

Her friend made no indication that she heard. She sank deeper, her statuesque legs disappearing a fraction of an inch at a time.

"Let her go," Fern said.

The imp only continued to smile as Julie sank. The water that swallowed Fern's friend seemed to be a sentient creature, eating Julie as if it thrived on her life force. The imp's blood-red smile spread wider.

The voice spoke in her mind. *You can save her.* He twirled the rope. *Die in her place.*

Was that the only way?

What meaning did death hold here?

Was it annihilation? Or something else?

More of Julie disappeared into the water. She was in up to her waist now. The look on her face was one of delicate ignorance, a catatonic daze.

Die in her place.

She trained the sharp stone on the imp, not sure if it would do him any harm, but not about to let her guard down. The imp continued twirling the rope in his hand. He mimed putting his head through the noose, and laughed without sound.

The bottom of Julie's ribcage sunk into the water. Pain contorted her face as she stirred from her trance.

You can save her. The imp shook the dangling noose and gestured for her to come forward.

Julie woke and screamed. She twisted and writhed as the water held her like tar. The sound of her screams made Fern's heart ache.

Save her.

Fern ran forward and grabbed the noose.

"Fern!" Julie screamed.

Fern gripped the noose, stepped onto a rock, and locked eyes with her friend. "I love you, Jules."

"Don't die for me. You don't have to!"

She brought the noose to her neck, preparing herself to

make a final leap into the unknown. She looked down, off the edge of the rock. *Do I really want to do this?* The imp pulled the rope toward her, tried to loop it around her neck. She squirmed to avoid the rope's grasp. *I need more time.* Time she didn't have.

The imp jumped from his perch and stalked toward her. She tried to use the rock to hold him at bay, but he snatched her wrist. His mouth opened wide as he pulled her closer. His breathing rose in volume, resembling an old machine, churning within him, churning within the walls of the cave. Engines of Ruin.

She stopped resisting. She went limp, except for her hold on the stone. He went to embrace her and pull her into his gaping maw. Inches from his swirling features, she jammed the stone into the back of his throat. As she used the heel of her hand to hammer the stone in deeper, she recited the poem's final lines. *And the Ruin will dry up and the souls will rise and all who love will be as one.* A gurgling scream exploded from his mouth. He released her and thrashed around the cave, his limbs and head striking rock walls.

She looked to the creek. Julie reached, the water up to her armpits. Maybe it wasn't Julie. Maybe it was her subconscious' way of shaping an ideal lover, but it looked like her, and in this world, wherever it was, that could be a start. Here Fern could remake things in her own image. She scooped up the rope and ran to the creek's edge.

"Julie, hang on!" She threw the rope into the water. The current pulled the rope down and yanked it from Fern's hand. "Fuck! Jules, can you…"

"I can't!" She was neck deep, close to joining others in the Ruin. Gray faces with mouths twisted into grimaces of agony, emaciated bodies writhing in sickness.

You can save her. The imp's voice in her head spoke in her head like the resurfacing memory of a schoolyard taunt.

Fern leapt into the water, into Julie's flailing embrace, and the Ruin washed over them. They sank. Violent current pushed them toward an unknown destination, but they held each other. The rushing of the water became so much like voices of the suffering. Fern felt the rope graze her leg and reached for it with her other hand. She wrapped it around her and Julie, bounding them together, against the harsh water.

They'd be down here forever. There was no other way this would end, she realized.

But they were together.

Maybe even in the Ruin that counted for something.

When she woke, Julie was gone.

The Last Easy Rider

On the weekend before I was to start my final semester at Texas State University, I used the leftover cash from my student loans plus money I'd saved from my summer job at my mother's law office to buy a 1969 Ford E-250 van that the previous owner swore would still run well, and I headed west, veins full of a red caffeinated river, teeth clenching every time the speedometer needle tipped over eighty. I suppose one could speculate on the triggering event that led to the exodus from the future I'd spent so many years meticulously planning and fervently working toward. They could lay the blame at the feet of my love affair with psychedelic drugs that mixed poorly with antidepressants, or the red-haired bad girl to whom I'd sacrificed what was left of my purity exactly one year after the priest who I looked to as a father figure throughout my tumultuous teenage years fucked me in the ass and told me that through his violation I had truly opened myself to the Spirit. They could also guess at what the ultimate goal of my travels was. They could say I was looking for myself or the American Dream or my ever absent yet perpetually present father. But the truth is that aside from an impulse that a more religious person than me would have called divine inspiration, nothing triggered this decision, and I was searching for nothing. I was no Kerouac and this was no Dennis Hopper-helmed misadventure that would end with my unceremonious assassination by disgruntled rednecks who didn't like my long hair. This was a trek across the American Void, but like the formless darkness that filled the universe before Father God and Mother Earth fucked life as we know it into existence, this Void was not empty.

The highways are full of demons. They lurk behind every death-defying curve and in the darkness of every mountain tunnel. They hang from white hilltop crosses, from tied and twisted star-spangled banners, and from roadside billboards for pornographic megastores. And not all of them are malignant; some are simply ghosts that have been dead so long they've forgotten to be human. But like ghosts they haunt me so.

They're all here: dark web cultists and the Lovecraftian gods they worship; the doomed preacher-turned-bartender who commits his own sins while trying to atone for those of others; the suicidal author who now resides in Our Lady of the Sea's icy arms; the married couple whose renewed vows are written in blood; the lovers on the run from their own private hells while all the world watches; the boy who buried his parents together with their demons because running away is never enough; Michaela and Eddie, now undead and wandering, always hungry, but together; the survivors of the sundered world and its cleansing fire; the documentarian searching for answers in murder cases no one else cares to remember; and Fern, ruined in her loneliness, all because she cared too much for everyone but herself. And they aren't the only ones here. And I'm not sure I'm still headed west. These highways are full of portals too. Not every exit ramp leads where it says it does. Sometimes directions are misleading. Sometimes when I go to sleep on the twin bed in the back of the van, I wake up somewhere else.

On the radio, people are calling it the end times, backwoods preachers and people of science alike singing the same doomsday song. But I keep on driving. I keep my lamp burning. Not because I'm waiting for Jesus, but because I'm a stubborn son of a bitch, with miles to go, in circles, out of time, across space both flat and 3D, in a world where television shows everything in vibrant high-definition, and real experiences blur into impressions the likes for which Monet would have earned both praise and derision.

These are my roads. This is my Void, and these creatures of the dark are mine to shine my light upon. I don't claim to have any answers; I couldn't possibly tell you how to navigate this primordial place. But I can listen. I can see. And I can report back.

All my love, from the nothingness of everything, yours truly, Lucas Mangum.

Author's Notes

I wrote "Ghost Music" specifically for this new edition. I'm very much interested in the idea of revisiting the past and unburying the sins that can be found beneath its grounds. I also love stories about rock stars. One of my favorite books is the highly embellished autobiography, *The Long Hard Road out of Hell*, by Marilyn Manson. I have a background in music, and despite being only a dabbler myself, I find stories of wretched excess can be quite cathartic. All of this converged to create the doomed character of Chase, who returns home to find his missing son, and ends up having to pay for the terrible things he's done.

The idea for "Hell and Back" came from two separate places. The first was a conversation I had with a religious former co-worker. While I don't remember how it came up, she said that it would be incredibly immoral for a former preacher to become a bartender. I disagreed; as I state in the story, being a preacher isn't so different from being a bartender. The second inspiration for this story came from my friends Dennis Tafoya and Don Lafferty, both authors themselves, who enjoyed my horror stories, but thought I should try my hand at writing crime fiction. "Hell and Back" was my way of accepting their challenge. I think I rose to the occasion quite nicely, but ultimately that's for you, reader, to decide.

For two summers in a row, my lovely wife, Jean, worked at the Jersey Shore locations for a grocery store chain. Understandably so, things got a lot busier during the summer months, and those stores needed all the help they could get. While visiting her one weekend, I wondered what these shore towns were like during the winter months. This was on my mind when Hurricane Sandy devastated the Jersey Shore during the fall of 2012. I was thinking about the evangelical talking point about storms being a punishment from the heavens. I was also thinking about the 1973 film, *The Wicker Man*. Somehow, the pieces came together and formed "Our Lady of the Sea."

"Worlds Colliding" was described by fellow horror writer, Brendan Vidito, as reminiscent of a European erotic thriller after I contributed the story to a chapbook I was releasing with him and Charles Austin Muir. That makes sense, in a lot of ways. I love European films. I love erotica. I love thrillers. Truth is, the story is partly inspired by actual events, though it's heavily embellished. A lot of times, I get my ideas by taking real situations from my life and asking, "what if *this* happened instead?" I came up with the idea for *Flesh and Fire* this way, but I think "Worlds Colliding" is a much stronger story.

I don't think I've ever worked so hard on a story as I did "Video Inferno." I wanted to write the literary equivalent of a David Lynch-inspired nightmare. Surreal fiction can sometimes seem like a lot of randomness, but really, if it's to be done well, it takes calculation. Oftentimes, one must put the piece away for months at a time and let it marinate. I think the version contained here is the closest I've come to what I wanted "Video Inferno" to be, but if I'm honest with myself, I don't think it will ever truly be done.

While "Offerings" is an older story of mine, I decided to include it in this new edition for two reasons. The first is that it's been significantly edited down from the amateurish version that appeared in the anthology, *crappy shorts: deuces wild*. The second again goes back to my affinity for stories about musicians. I sometimes feel like I didn't make the right decision when I abandoned my musical pursuits, but getting to live these lives through telling these types of stories is a worthy consolation.

My inspirations for this story were Skipp and Spector's seminal novel, *The Scream,* and the previously mentioned autobiography of Marilyn Manson.

Coming from Bucks County, a vast Philadelphia suburb populated with woods and farmland, haunted hayrides were a Halloween tradition for my friends and me. They came to embody a childish innocence for me, despite the macabre imagery, so for the story, "Hayride," I came to imagine a twenty-something having an existential crisis, revisiting a place that had brought him much joy throughout his life, with the intention of killing himself there. Whether the little boy he encounters on the hayride that night is a ghost or not remains unclear to me, though Howard's fate is certain. I'm sure he'll be okay, at least for a while.

"Worm Magic" started off as a short screenplay. Funny thing about making movies though? You usually need to find other people to make them with you. Writing the script is the easy part. After that, if you plan to do things independently, you have to coordinate schedules, come up with money, and figure out how to feed people who are gracious enough to work for you. I have not the slightest amount of experience doing any of this, and as a parent of a toddler, as well as being a full-time student and part-time writer, I frankly don't have the time to learn. That said, I really enjoyed this story. I enjoyed it so much, I couldn't stand the idea of not letting it find its way into the world. As headache-inducing as organizing a film shoot would be for me, turning my little script into a little story was pure pleasure. This writing stuff can be a lot of fun sometimes, and in the case of "Worm Magic," it was especially true.

"Occupy Babylon" was born out of the Occupy Wall Street protests of 2011. They were all over the news at the time. I was also caught up in the *Walking Dead* phenomenon, much like the rest of the world. I wanted to tell a zombie story set during similar protests, only in times even more apocalyptic than these. I needed a catalyst though. My catalyst came in the form of a religious conversion and a rumor that a dangerous zealot had taken over the Philly contingent of the Occupy protests. There was also the matter of seeing Scout Tafoya's brilliant zombie film, *The Last Flesh and Blood Show*. All of this percolated in my head until the entire story came to me in the shower one morning, and I put it to paper over the following few days.

My mentor, Jonathan Maberry, has often said that the best zombie stories are not about zombies. "The World Asunder" is a zombie story without zombies in it. Funny thing, I kept expecting them to show up, even thought about expanding the story past its logical conclusion so I could include them, but after much honest reflection, I decided to leave the story as it was. It didn't need zombies to show up, even though they factored much into the backstory. The character of Kyle was frightening enough, I think.

"A Killing Back Home" came from a conversation with author and editor, Leza Cantoral, who posed that my style would be well-suited in the murder mystery genre. I wanted a challenge and had an idea kicking around in my head that I thought would work. The story has been one of my most successful. It's been downloaded over five-hundred times and it's been optioned for film. Not bad for a first-time mystery writer, huh?

If "Video Inferno" was the most difficult story to write, "Waters of Ruin" comes in a close second. Its initial incarnation was a 12,000-word novelette. I whittled it down, cutting useless scenes and adding subtle layers. What I wanted was a dreamlike story, but it still had to read like a story. It still had to make sense. Several drafts later, it has taken what I believe is its final form. And it makes sense. At least I think so.

"The Last Easy Rider" is less a short story, and more of a manifesto. I wrote it in a frenzy, on my cellphone, after conjuring the image of myself in an old camper van traveling the American highways. Writing it felt like such an honest expression of what was swimming around in my subconscious that, while I know few of its words are true, I have a hard time telling where reality ends and the fiction begins. If that sounds pretentious, I assure you that it is not. I believe there are other dimensions than the one we know, and I believe that sometimes we can access them.

This collection wouldn't have been possible without the assistance from some great editors and pre-readers. Special thanks to: Jack Bantry, Chris Bauer, Eric S. Brown, Leza Cantoral, Nathan Crowder, Patrick Galloway, Paul Goblirsch, Brian Keene, Don Lafferty, Ruth Littner, Jonathan Maberry, Jean Mangum, Vincent Mangum, Lisa Mannetti, Jon McGoran, Shane McKenzie, Charles Austin Muir, J. David Osborne, Alyssa Padilla, Greg Schauer, Dennis Tafoya, Scout Tafoya, Brendan Vidito, and David Niall Wilson.

About the Author

L ucas Mangum is the author of *Flesh and Fire, Gods of the Dark Web,* and *We Are the Accused.* He currently resides in Austin with his family. Subscribe at patreon.com/LMangumFiction for new content every month.

Curious about other Crossroad Press books?
Stop by our site:
http://store.crossroadpress.com
We offer quality writing
in digital, audio, and print formats.

Enter the code FIRSTBOOK
to get 20% off your first order from our store!
Stop by today!

www.ingramcontent.com/pod-product-compliance
Lightning Source LLC
Chambersburg PA
CBHW061236170626
46809CB00007B/2696